HANGTREE RANGE

Now that the cattle barons and the sheepherders had declared open war, there could be no peace until one side owned the range. They lived and fought by one code: take what you want and kill anyone who tries to take it away. On one side was cattleman Lem Cooley, who had been spilling blood for thirty years so his cattle could roam free. Facing him was sheepherder Halliburton, who had done plenty of killing himself. Guns wouldn't settle the score—they needed the heavy branches of the Hangman's Tree. . .

HANGTREE RANGE

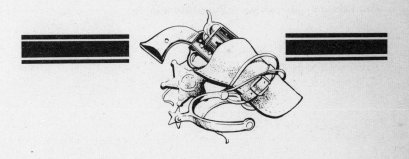

William Hopson

ATLANTIC LARGE PRINT
Chivers Press, Bath, England.
John Curley & Associates Inc.,
South Yarmouth, Mass., USA.

Library of Congress Cataloging-in-Publication Data

Hopson, William.
  Hangtree range.

  "Atlantic large print."
  1. Large type books.   I. Title.
[PS3515.O6526H3   1986]   813'.54   85–27583
ISBN 0–89340–276–1 (J. Curley: lg. print)

British Library Cataloguing in Publication Data

Hopson, William.
  Hangtree range.—Large print ed.—
  (Atlantic large print)
  I. Title
  813'.54[F]   PS3515.O6526

  ISBN 0–7451–9183–5

This Large Print edition is published by Chivers Press, England, and
John Curley & Associates, Inc, U.S.A. 1986

Published by arrangement with Donald MacCampbell, Inc

U.K. Hardback ISBN 0 7451 9183 5
U.S.A. Softback ISBN 0 89340 276 1

HANGTREE RANGE

CHAPTER ONE

In Wilcox that afternoon the usual group of idlers and cowpunchers from outlying ranches were in their favorite place, in the shade of George Hand's saloon; watching the experts at horseshoe pitching try to beat perennial rivals, and sometimes betting on the results. Through the open side door Ed Allen, reading a newspaper back of the bar, could hear the laughter, the excited shouts, and more often the good-natured jeers. Now and then a man would get up from his haunches and come inside to have his goblet filled with ice cold beer.

The man who did that now was Poke Saunders, an easygoing, angular man of forty, who made his living by helping to load cattle over at the railroad shipping pens.

'Guess I'll take another, Ed,' he said, shoving the big glass over the bar. 'We got to load a big bunch of stuff at daylight, and I might as well be cool while I can. Anything in that paper about the cattle-sheep war up in Apache Basin?'

Allen said, 'Somebody really hung that fellow Parker from Texas, all right. That much is known for sure by the sheriff, who's

1

afraid of both factions. He's from the Mexican settlement of San Marino, which means that Lem Cooley and the sheepmen of Johnathan Breuger will go on killing without interference from the law. Well ... Breuger knew the risk when he put ninety thousand head of his Colorado sheep through the Mogollons and into Apache Basin for summer range. He knows the cowmen risked their lives and their families' lives at the hands of the Apaches to hold that land, and he must have known Cooley's reputation as a tough old fighter.'

He pushed the refilled goblet over to Poke and picked up the nickel. He was a medium-sized man of thirty-one, blond and with a honey-colored mustache, full but carefully trimmed; a man who was mild-mannered and quiet and very highly regarded in the town of Wilcox.

He said, 'The law should handle that ugly mess up there because, legally, Breuger has it on his side, Poke. That's why most of the ranchers are afraid to fight. All except Cooley, who's fought savagely and without mercy all his life.'

As a former scout, he knew of Cooley and the country involved, for just the year before, in 1886, Geronimo the Apache renegade had surrendered himself and his thirty-odd warriors to General Miles and the more than

2

five thousand troops it had been necessary to use to run down the wily raider. This was the final handful of hostiles out, all the others—about four thousand five hundred in number—being on the reservation. And the surrender had ended forever the Apache wars against the whites in Arizona Territory. Except for the usual number of outlaws and badmen found in any part of the cow country in 1887, Arizona was now a safe country that was growing and prospering fast.

And on the same day that Geronimo wrote finis to decades of bloody fighting and raiding, Ed Allen had drawn his pay and come to Wilcox with three years' savings as scout, interpreter, and packer. Like old Geronimo, he was writing finis to an era in his life. He wanted to build solidly for the future in a community that was growing fast, where the average man now found it unnecessary to pack a heavy gun and shell belt while in town from the ranges.

Ed had known George Hand for a good many years, the old pioneer's adobe saloon being virtual headquarters for the cattlemen and their men while in town. Ed had gone to work for him as night bartender and then, three months later, bought a half-interest in the place. Old George usually opened up at five in the morning so that any of the men

3

starting to load cattle at daylight who wanted an early morning 'picker-upper' could get one. Ed Allen usually took over around four in the afternoon and remained open as long as business warranted, which quite often was all night. In his off hours he worked methodically and painstakingly to shape and dry and then to lay the adobe bricks that were forming the thick walls of what one day would be a big, sprawling six-room home with a *ramada* all the way around it.

Poke took a long cool swallow and put down his glass. 'Uh-huh, you're plumb right about the whole business, Ed. Them sheepmen not only got the law and even men in Washington on their side; they also got money to burn, where them cowmen are pore as Job's turkey. If it wasn't for the way sheep ruin a range, I'd git some sense, was I them cattlemen, and run sheep. But they're too stubborn to take a one hundred percent profit on each sheep each year like Breuger does; old Lem in particular. I don't go around much talkin' about other men behind their backs. Don't believe in it. But there never was a meaner, more vicious man ever lived than Lem Cooley.'

Ed shrugged and picked up his paper again. He said, 'Nobody knows it any better than that sheep baron. That's why he sent down Halliburton in charge. They don't come any tougher. Oh, well, just as long as they keep it up there.'

George Hand came waddling in out of the white heat from the café across the street, punching through his white mustache with a toothpick. He was short, heavy-bellied, pudgy-fisted, and still strong at seventy-three; reserve strength stored up from a life in the open. It had been exactly fifty years ago, in the year 1837, that Hand had come into the country of the then friendly Apaches as a trapper. He was trapping when Johnson, the renegade Englishman, invited the Apaches to a gathering to receive gifts, and then blew women and children and warriors to bits with a hidden howitzer loaded with nails and bolts and rocks to get the scalps. Mexicans, unable to cope with the raiders, were paying fifty gold pesos for a baby's scalp, one hundred for a woman's, one hundred and fifty for a warrior's.

That was the beginning of the Apache wars against the whites. They killed a party of trappers the very afternoon of the tragedy, and a second party the following morning; only one man escaped. George Hand was now seventy-three. He said, 'Ready to pull out together, Ed?'

Ed Allen closed the paper and nodded. 'My pack is over in my shack. I'll fool that young

5

pup brother of mine. He sent word by a Mexican liquor smuggler that I was too soft to get out of the shade long enough to ride down and meet him somewhere on Arroyo Seco tomorrow afternoon. One gets you five I'll find the little cuss in Tony Moreno's adobe bar drinking up all the tequila and mescal in the place,' he added, and grinned.

He knew that ornery, grinning kid brother of his too well.

Bill was the youngest of the four Allen brothers, two of them ranching in the San Saba country of Texas; a joyous, insouciant, rambunctious youngster without a care in the world except a lovely sixteen-year-old Spanish girl.

At fourteen Bill Allen had run away from the ranch in Texas and followed Ed to Wilcox where the older Allen was working and learning from George Hand the Apache language Hand's young Apache wife had taught him nearly fifty years before, shortly before dying of consumption. At fifteen Bill Allen had seen the six-horse coach of Don Alphonso Perez y Estrada in the streets of Wilcox one day and the dark eyes of a young *señorita* and the angry, suspicious eyes of her *dueña* staring at him; one pair excited, the other pair scolding. At sixteen Bill Allen was riding with Don Alphonso's vaqueros and

6

speaking Spanish like a native. At nineteen he was slated to become the rich Don's *Americano* son-in-law.

'You going down to Mexico for that big wedding of hisn this fall?'

'I'll have to,' Ed grinned. 'Joe and Mike are bringing their families all the way from the home ranch. It ought to be quite an occasion.'

Hand removed the toothpick and spat and wiped his mustache with a sleeve. He said seriously, 'I ain't so sure I want to see you go, dang it, Ed. You might get down there and see what the kid is marryin' into—such as forty-five thousand head of cattle—and begin lookin' around to see if the old Don ain't got another daughter or two. I don't want to lose a good business pardner. I want to quit in a couple or three more years when my feet finally play out, and sell you my share. Then I want to sit back and watch you grow with this town. You're one man who believes that you can't drink likker and sell the stuff too. You work hard and save your money and don't make enemies even when you have to stop a fight between a couple of cowpunchers now and then, and people respect you.'

Allen got off the stool and drew a tall glass of cold water from a wooden barrel with chunks of ice in it. He drank and said, 'No fear, George. I know what I want, and it's

7

here. The way I figure it, Bill is a good kid who's getting a lot of fun out of life while he's still young and single. Once he settles down to helping the old Don handle half the state of Sonora and Chihuahua, he'll be all right, and I might be able to get in on some of the cattle they'll ship through here.'

'But in the meantime yo're gettin' itchy feet just the same to git back in a saddle, hey?'

'Something like that,' Ed admitted, and began washing the glass. 'I'll take a pack outfit down, meet the kid, maybe do a little prospecting for a couple of days to get some outdoor chuck under my belt again, and we'll come on in.'

Hand asked the same question that Poke had asked. 'Anything in the paper about that cattle-sheep war way up there in Apache Basin?'

'They didn't mention the Burton brothers. Probably afraid to.'

From outside the open door there came a loud yell of laughter and a whoop, and a half-dozen laughing men came pushing inside and up to the bar to settle a beer bet somebody had lost. Ed served them, and when things had quieted down Poke spoke to George Hand.

'George, you knowed old Lem Cooley a long time, him and them Burtons, didn't you?'

8

Hand nodded and eased his broad seat onto his own special stool at the end of the bar. 'Yep, I knew him and the Burtons when they was kids. Old man Burton was killed right there where you're standin', 'bout six year ago now, I guess. And I saw the man who killed him. See that old Apache rifle up there above the bar? He traded that in here for a quart of whiskey, got drunk, and got shot that night.'

'Them Burton boys were born on old Cooley's ranch, wasn't they, George?' asked another of the now quiet men.

'Yep, they was little kids the mornin' Victoria and his 'Paches cut in on the ranch and got the tar whipped outen them. Old Burton was up on top as lookout, like Lem always had a man there, and he killed the first one. He took that old smooth-bore rifle up there above the mirror, an' when him an' his Mexican woman and them two boys moved to Wilcox, he brought it along. He loafed around town here for years, makin' a livin' somehow or other, while them two boys growed up. They were tough little cusses, and I ain't sayin' they had anything to do with the lynching of thet Texan named Parker up in the basin. I just wouldn't be surprised if the reports didn't turn out to be true. But that's their business, boys, just as long as they don't show up in Wilcox an' git that blasted war

9

mixed up with us folks down here. It's their fight, an' I hope nobody of us in this part of the country will git hurt on account of it. Well, Ed,' rising from the stool and rubbing at the seat of his trousers, 'I think I'll sleep a little while this evenin' and come in at midnight to relieve you in case there's still some business around. See you later.'

CHAPTER TWO

South of Wilcox, toward the Mexican border, the Arizona desert spreads out into a great panorama of low rolling hills covered with sparse vegetation fighting for existence in a land often baked by a blazing sun. A land cut and slashed by arroyos, most of them rain-made during flash floods, and then becoming dry and barren and gravel-covered. At one particular spot an underground stream had pushed its labored way to the surface and meandered away, following a twisting course to the south; and some man long dead, and probably with a sense of frontier humor, had named it Arroyo Seco—Dry Creek. It cut its wet path for a distance of more than one hundred miles down through the dry, pitiless desert heat, the wide belt of cottonwood trees—which the Mexicans called Alamos—making it cool even in July. A long, sinuous belt of green; a magnet that had drawn first the wild early day Apaches in their peregrinations from one place to another, the first trappers, then the pioneer cattlemen and their long-haired riders, followed by prospectors and desperadoes. Soldiers trailing renegade Apaches had camped there, and a posse of men from the pueblo city of Tucson had once shot it out with a band of outlaws hidden in ambush in the brush along the east bank.

Birds twittered among the cottonwoods; carefree and contented except when the big hawks, hunting a sundown supper before going to roost, suddenly came smashing down through the branches with outstretched talons to snare and fly off with tiny feathered victims whose shrieks soon were stilled by one vicious blow of a razor-sharp beak.

The birds were twittering now, and just as suddenly became still as sound came out of the shimmering heat waves on the slope of the desert above. The birds waited a few moments and then flew away as the two horsemen came into view and trotted into the welcome shade of the cottonwoods.

They pulled up by a mighty tree so old that all of its limbs except one had, down through the years, broken from overweight and fallen, leaving great gashes on the scarred trunk; in turn to be carried away, tumbling and twisting, when the heavy spring rains turned the creek into a raging torrent of brown water.

They were born to the desert, these two swarthy-faced riders. You could tell it by their boots, scuffed and scarred from walking in sand and among rocks instead of grass. It was in the thorn marks on their leather chaps and saddles, where at one time or another they had fought the wild cattle, working at the most hellish cowpunching job in any section of the great American cattle ranges: in the Arizona brush country; among thorny mesquites, great towering cacti, and the deadly *cholla*, hell's own diabolical contribution to the Arizona desert. That was the reason for the smaller hats, sugar-cured to make the brims lie flat against a man's head; so necessary working in thick, thorny brush. One of the horses had a swollen, angry-looking spot on one shoulder; a spot where scores of those vicious little *cholla* thorns had been extracted and others left to fester so they could be removed later.

They sat there for a few moments with their hats off, wiping at swarthy faces covered with a month's growth of pitch black hair, the color inherited from their Mexican mother. For these were the Burton brothers, born on old Lem Cooley's ranch; sometimes cowpunchers at wilderness roundups that the Mexicans called rodeos, sometimes cattle thieves, and now suspected killers for the invading Breuger sheep interests.

Frank Burton, the older brother, replaced his odd-looking, dirty hat and looked at Stub. 'Well, kid, looks like that two-hundred-and-fifty-mile circle down here put us in the clear. We made it.'

'We sho' traveled far enough,' grinned back Stub. 'Even if they found thet Texan right after we swung him, I figger the wind covered our tracks enough so they could never trail us, especially when we rode a split trail sixty miles apart and then rendezvooed at Stinking Springs. Let's water these hosses, and then it's me fer some of it, too.'

They gigged the tired horses away from the tree and down a six-foot sand bank that caved and was left gashed. The water, four inches deep and coursing slowly over the smooth sandy bottom, was crystal clear, and the tiny fish darted away, gone in a flash as the two thirsty animals sank their warm, dry muzzles and began to suck big swallows. Stub took an empty canteen, unscrewed the cap, and lowered it by the leather strap to let it run partly full.

'You think,' he asked, straightening with the dripping object in his hands, 'thet we could risk a trip to Wilcox? I'd sorta like to see what the old place looks like since you shot Willie Agens in George Hand's saloon fer killing the old man six year ago.'

'All depends,' replied Frank. 'If we knowed that word of the hangin' hasn't got down this way yet, and we wasn't suspected, I'd like to take a chanct. But the hull trouble is that them sheepmen have got the law on their side, even though Breuger's tough sheep foreman did pay us to do the job. He's tough, thet Halliburton. Be a hull lot better either to hole up in some town where we ain't knowed or keep on hitting for the border. Here—gimme a shot at thet canteen and don't be such a hawg. I'm as dry as you are. Wisht we had something stronger to drink.'

Stub handed over the dripping canteen and chuckled. 'Don't worry, boy. With two hundred and fifty cartwheels apiece in our pockets, we'll have it, and lots, pretty soon. I still think I shoulda shot Tracy and took his share. If they ketch him he'll squeal like a *javalina* boar pig shot in the rump with bird shot.'

He pulled up his mount's head, reined around, and sent it scrambling back up the damp sandy bank. Frank followed, and they

14

both swung from leather. Stub was stripping off his gunbelt and chaps while gazing up at the tree with its lone remaining limb. Frank said suddenly, 'Hey, look, Stub! Over there a little ways. A grave, shore as shootin'.'

They walked over through the deep sand to where what once had been an oblong mound was now gradually succumbing to wind and rain and beginning to flatten out again. When the floods came early the following year, there would be no evidence of the grave left after their passing.

'Yep, it's a grave, all right. I'll bet you five of this two hundred and fifty sheep money in my pocket thet somebody done to him what we done to thet back-shootin' Texan. I don't know what this gent done, but if he was a Texan like them two Parkers, I hope they hung him high. I reckon Pete will be plumb upset when he finds his pore cousin, hey?'

Frank said a little grimly, 'It'll be a long time before they call us "greasers" again just because our old lady was a Mexican.'

'Ron Parker anyhow,' agreed Stub.

He turned and retraced his way to his horse, noticed the swollen spot on its shoulder, and reached into a pocket for his jackknife. He opened a blade with a needle point, ran his exploring hand over the festered lump, and went to work on the flinching mount,

15

removing more of the almost invisible *cholla* spikes.

'Serves you right,' he told the quivering animal. 'You'd oughta had better sense than to spook at a jack-rabbit and brush into a *cholla*. Here I go and use a spade bit on you, the dirtiest, cuttin'est bit ever put in a horse's mouth, just so's you'll learn to rein away fast from cactus—and I'm blamed if you don't spook right *into* one. Maybe you'll get some sense some day, but I doubt it.'

Stark naked, Frank Burton lunged forward, gunbelt in hand, and jumped from sight over the soft sandy bank, his swarthy, almost black body gleaming. He was tall where Stub was short; lean where Stub was stocky. He'd always made coarse, guffawing remarks on the fact that he was lean like their *Americano* old man while Stub was just a short, fat Mexican like their mother. He placed the gunbelt on a grey cottonwood limb half buried in the sand at the water's edge and leaped in and fell flat; threshing his legs in the four inches of water like a small boy in swimming for the first time.

Stub came plunging in after him and they lay there, cooling their dark, hard bodies, their skins showing marks of thorns, rope burns, and the scar of a knife cut on Frank's slender back. The evening was becoming a little cooler now, though out on the slopes of the desert the heat waves still shimmered and would do so until sundown. The horses remained motionless, tired after covering more than forty miles, eyes closed. The birds had returned and were noisy again.

Stub Burton sat up and began to rub himself with wet sand. He said, 'I'm still wonderin' if old man Cooley has found Parker's carcass yet where we left it swingin' from the limb of that jack pine.'

'Must have,' his brother grunted. 'But finding him an' provin' thet we done it is bobcats of two different colors. Nobody knows that Halliburton hired us to do the job. Just us four. They ain't got no proof if it went to court. But one thing you can bet yore saddle on. Parker won't back-shoot any more Chihuahua sheepherders!' He broke off into gusty laughter. 'Ol' Bud Tracy was sure scared, wa'nt he?'

'He sure as the devil was,' grinned Stub Burton. 'Him a-braggin' and a-blowin' all week while he hunted thet Texan's camp about what *he* was gonna do when we caught him. Then hollering because we used his riata. Didja see how his hands was tremblin' when he put on thet noose?'

They went off into gales of laughter, remembering Lem Cooley and their childhood

17

days on the fierce old man's ranch. That was what had made it so funny: being raised on the old devil's place and then ending up taking sheep money to hang one of Lem's hired killers of sheepherders.

Frank rose to his feet and squeezed out his dripping black whiskers. He stiffened as one of the horses lifted a slumped hip and flicked its ears forward. The head of the other, hanging low, came up high, and it too perked up its ears. Frank moved instinctively.

He bounded through the water and snatched up his gunbelt and sprinted for the protection of the bank while he slipped the .44 that once had belonged to his father from the sheath. Stub, wet sand clinging to his stocky young body, was beside him, peering.

'Somebody coming,' whispered Frank. 'Get our saddle guns. Quick!'

He half crouched, half lay there, as naked as the day his mother had borne him. The water made his shaggy, coarse black hair glisten like the sheen of a skunk's fur; and his face, had it been shaven, would have been not at all unhandsome. It wasn't a particularly mean-looking or cruel-looking face; it even had much courage and determinaton. Right now there was animal wariness in the coal black eyes.

He thought, Well, the old man always said

18

we'd never come to no good. But then neither did he, and I wonder what ever happened to the old lady after Stub and me left Wilcox?

Overhead a big black buzzard floated by on silent wings, and a snatch from an old Mexican song came into his mind. *El Zopilote Mojado*. The Wet Buzzard. Now just why in the blazes, he thought, am I thinking of that? Oh, I know now. Got to thinking of the old man, so naturally I'd think of the old lady. Guess she's hooked up with some Mexican by now. I'll have to find out one of those days if we ever get back to Wilcox. She hugged me in her fat black arms while Stub sat on the floor and squalled the day the old duck helped Lem Cooley stand off Victoria and his Apaches after they hit the ranch. Stub was really bawling like fury, while I was hollering to go out and see the fight.

It all came back vividly to Frank Burton as he lay there covered with wet sand and watched his younger brother jerking the carbines out of their scabbards. From the roof above and all around the fortress-like building he could hear the sound of firing, the screaming of the terrified Mexican women, the crying of the children.

His fat *Mamacita* had said, 'Hush, or the Apaches will get you.'

'Where are they? I want to go out and see.'

19

'Stop yelling and trying to pull away or I'll spank your bottom. You can go out later, Francisco, when they are gone. Listen to the guns and the yelling and be quiet before I slap you.'

He thought, Yeah, I remember the old man toddling me out to let me look at the dead one and to pick up the rifle. He was as black as the ace of spades except where the blood ran out of his neck into the sand. The old duck sure got him dead center. Had a white streak painted across his face right below the eyes. Don't know how he ever hit anything with that smooth-bore muzzle loader the old man later traded to George Hand in Wilcox for a quart of whiskey, before he himself got killed by Willie Agens. Willie was some surprised when I tailed him into Hand's saloon the next day and faced him with the old duck's six-shooter, this same one I've got right here in my hand.

'How come you shot the old duck, Willie?'

'He was drunk and I thought he was a-goin' to pull a gun on me. So I just pulled mine out and cut him down through the belly, that's all. I hope you ain't mad, Frank.'

'Me? Why, not at all, Willie. A man has a right to pertect himself. What I'm so plumb upset about is that after you put one into his belly you wouldn't let nobody touch him till

20

he died. Just like I'm going to do to you, Willie. Nope, it won't do you no good to beg, but you can go for your gun while I got you lined if you want to. I like to give a man a fair chanct. How do you like it down there on the floor, Willie? What are you kicking and hollering so loud about, Willie? Why don't you get up off the floor and have a drink with me, Willie?'

No, Frank Burton thought, he couldn't get up, blast him. Not with a slug from the old duck's forty-four right in the middle of his navel. It must have gone in and stopped somewhere against the backbone, though he could still kick and scream and hold both hands over his bloody shirt front. 'You boys just stay right where you are, because if you don't I'll kill the first man who tries to help him. I want him to feel like the old duck felt. George, you might as well give me a beer to kill time until Willie stops kicking. If he ain't through by then I'll put another one—no? All right. I can do without it, I reckon. *El Zopilote Majado*. Why, I'm all covered with sand and look like a wet black buzzard myself!'

Stub came sprinting barefooted back from the horses, a short-barrel carbine in each wet hand. They were .44–40's, model of 1867, using the same cartridge as Frank's inherited

21

six-shooter. Stub jumped over the bank.

'What the devil are you grinning for and humming the old Wet Buzzard song?' he demanded incredulously. 'Have you gone loco? You pick the doggonedest times to get funny.'

'Just thinking, my lad, just thinking. You're too young to understand. Some day when you grow up and can dress yourself without me helping you, I'll tell you all about it. What do you suppose ever become of the old lady after all?'

'Shut up! You see anything yet?'

'Not yet. But whatever it is, it's coming. Look at them hosses over there under that tree.'

Both mounts now stood with stiffened forelegs, ears pointed forward, reins dragging. A faint breeze had sprung up and begun to rustle the green leaves of the lone big limb above the horses where the birds carried on their domestic life. Far to the west a giant whirlwind had leaped up and was twisting and slashing its way across the hot, arid rock slope of the desert's floor, its funnelling yellow plume high in the sky.

Frank Burton pulled down the lever on his .44–40, made sure of the brass shell in the chamber, closed it again and cocked the hammer. He said, 'Here it comes. One hoss at least and mebbeso more. Don't shoot until I give the word.'

CHAPTER THREE

During the six years that Frank Burton had found it expedient to keep away from Wilcox because of the Willie Agens murder, a couple of new revolutions such as always seemed to be breaking out sporadically down in Mexico had flared up. And in one of these outbursts of the cruelly subjugated peons against their masters, *Capitan* Antonio Moreno had at last lost control of his long-smoldering indignation. He tore off his insignia of rank and became a leader of the peons and *Indios*.

Like all others of the period, this one was short and bloody and disastrous for the *revoltosos*.

Pitchforks and machetes and bare feet were no match for the well mounted militia armed with guns, and the result was a deliberate and ruthless slaughter. In the thick of the melee an officer bearing down upon a fleeing peon, with lance poised to run him through, saw his former fellow officer rise up out of a brush clump, pistol in hand. That was the last thing he saw before the apologetic Moreno's bullet struck. Moreno mounted the dead man's horse, resigned his commission as general on the spot, and decided that habitation north of the border would be more pleasant as well as conducive to a longer span of life. He paused long enough to return to his former compound, now practically deserted because of the fight; and while the few guards left behind slept off a drunk, he leisurely looted the quarters of his fellow officers, including the unfortunate man whose horse he now rode.

Being of a practical turn of mind, the ex-general of the peons thoughtfully picked up and took along a very pretty girl of fifteen who, up until now, he had been unable to take as a spouse because of the differences in their social strata. This formality being taken care of by the priest at Don Alphonso Perez y Estrada's sprawling hacienda headquarters with its three hundred people, the ex-captain, ex-general rode northward with his happy bride to the land of the *norteamericanos*.

They struck the Arroyo Seco at the border of Arizona Territory, and inasmuch as the legality of his sudden resignation from the Mexican Army might be questioned, with subsequent inquiries of the American Cavalry, the now plain *Señor* Antonio Moreno wisely decided that it might be best to change his name.

'We are Americans now, my darling,' he told the pretty girl atop the bobbing pack containing, among other things, no small fortune in gold and silver and jewelry. He had felt little compunction in taking these things, for most of the officers, unlike himself, were strutting young rooster sons of rich *haciendados* and therefore enemies of the peons, to whose number *Señor* Moreno had belonged for a brief period of three days.

'Therefore,' he went on, 'now that we are Americans we must have an American name. I regret giving up the honored old one, but fortune smiles on us, my dove, because it just so happens that our name of Moreno in Spanish means Brown in English. A brown object, my love. Henceforth, you shall be *La Señora* Margarita Brown. I shall be *El Señor* Antonio Moreno—I mean I'll be Tony Brown.'

As a carefree and happy bridegroom—though the formality had, through insurmountable obstacles, been a few months late—as well as now a very, very rich one compared to former standards, on his honeymoon Tony followed the winding course of the Arroyo Seco for thirty miles northward before its course in that direction made an abrupt change and turned due west for nearly a mile before again resuming in a northerly

25

direction. This wide expanse of creek bottom sloped back from the water bed for more than a quarter of a mile to higher ground, and it was here that Tony decided to stay. It was an ideal place for a ranch.

With native sagacity Tony buried his wealth, set up camp, and began the building of his monster adobe cabin.

In time the low, flat-roofed building was finished, and around it soon flourished gardens and corn and flowers—and with it came the doom of Tony's hopes as a rancher. Riders began to drop by, and custom demanded that they be fed; outlaws, saddle tramps, desert prospectors, now and then a posse. Good-hearted Tony fed them all and justifiably felt increasing alarm. He was about to be eaten out of a home.

Being of a practical turn of mind because of his former station in life, he quickly supplied a remedy by building a bar and then freighting in from distant Tucson loads of supplies to sell to the visitors while they paid for the good Mexican food prepared by his hard-working wife and drank the tequila and mescal he paid to have smuggled in from Mexico. He was in business under a crudely lettered sign over the front door: The Alamo. Five years later Alamo was a small settlement of perhaps a dozen adobe cabins, and Tony Brown was a quiet, thoughtful businessman who took the money of those who came in and asked no questions.

On this particular afternoon Tony stood back of the short bar in the adobe coolness of the big room, talking with the former Reverend Samuel Ernest. Ernest was a well educated, friendly, sincere man who had come west to the desert to wait for the rest of his weak lungs to rot out and then to die in peace and obscurity, answering the call of the Big Fellow to come on across the Line and give Him a hand because it was a big job and a lot of help was needed. He was probably forty years of age, slightly bald, and with the unmistakable stoop of those similarly afflicted. He had determinedly set about to build his own adobe cabin under Tony's expert advice and supervision, a few minutes at a time between rest pauses, until the job was done without help. In between he made his own furniture of cottonwood and green rawhide, planted his own lush garden, and then one day 'Parson,' as the men jokingly referred to him, discovered that perhaps that Big Fellow didn't need his help after all. He wasn't going to die right now, nor for quite some time to come.

A half-dozen desert riders sat around talking, as they drank the smuggled liquor which also was Tony's acquisition, telling news of everything of importance happening in towns as far north as Wilcox and Tucson and as far south as *La Ciudad de Chihuahua*—Chihuahua City.

Tony was saying to the 'Parson,' and paying no attention to the talk of the others, 'Look, Sam, I run a tough joint through circumstances that just sort of happened. I tried by the sword to right a little of the injustices of my people and it turned into a tragic fizzle—and don't blame me for using that word fizzle because I got it from you while you taught me to perfect my English. I came up here across the border intending to start a ranch, use it as a place of refuge for other officers like myself, and then one day go back home and knock the tar out of the Government with some peon armies and get the poor devils some justice. I wound up running this joint for money, somewhere along the line having lost my devotion to God. But you're different. You still have it, and I think that's pretty good proof that that Big Fellow, as you call him, made you well and wants you to get back to work. Seems to me He had things pretty well figured out. You thought He wanted you to come on across the Line and give him a hand. Looks like He wants you to do that all right, but to do it

28

down here for a while. I may sound like a damned preacher—wup, sorry, Sam! I mean why don't you get out of this stink hole and get back to work?'

Ernest smiled at the serious expression on Tony's face, listening to the squalling yell of an infant back in the big combination kitchen and dining room. He said, 'I don't think that you've lost as much devotion as you imagine, Tony. There must have been some of that Big Fellow left inside of you when you found me coughing out my lungs and half dead from starvation in a Mexican shack in Wilcox. You saved a life for the Big Fellow. You saved it a second time when that small party of Apache bucks struck at this place three years ago. But you're right about me going back to Ohio. I belong back there in a parsonage, with a flock to guide and to help with their troubles. So now that there is peace over this once bloody land, I'll be saddling up my old mare one of these days very soon and riding into town. I can sell her for enough train fare to get back home.'

'You won't need money—' Tony began, and then broke off as a man came in from the white glare of the sun outside; a middle-aged rider from a ranch over in the Verde Springs valley. He leaned against the bar and removed his hat to wipe at his forehead.

'Hello, Bert,' Tony greeted him. 'Haven't seen you for a couple or three weeks. What'll it be?'

'A big snort of tequila with a great big glass of cool water first,' the man Bert said. 'And then some cut plug.' He turned casually and nodded greetings to the men, most of whom he knew.

Tony brought the water from a huge clay *olla* swinging from the ceiling and poured out the colorless fiery liquor. He said, 'Kinda hot, eh?'

Bert nodded and drank most of the water and wiped at his lips before attacking the tequila. He picked up a salt shaker, licked the back of his hand wet, poured on the salt, licked it into his mouth, then downed the raw liquor at a gulp and followed it with the rest of the water.

Tony said, 'Anything new over your way?'

'The old man got back from Wilcox in his buggy about noon. Says there's a big cattle-sheep war broke loose up in Apache Basin near the Mogollons. You heard anything about it?'

Tony shrugged. 'One of the pack trains came through today and brought yesterday's paper. Two sheepherders, imported from Mexico by that German, Breuger, got killed up there some time ago, and then the man

30

who's supposed to have done it was found hanging from a tree. That's about all we know.'

'The old man says there's some talk of the ranchers up there asking Cattle Association members down here to send up some guns to help old Lem Cooley carry on his lone hand fight. In other words, they're afraid of the law and won't fight, but they'll hire men.'

It had gotten quiet in the room, the men sitting in studied casualness, listening. A man who had been drinking rather heavily got up from his chair and came over; a loutish-looking man of about twenty-three with hulking shoulders. He was Joe Beckum, a Texan who had fled San Saba County, and was now wanted back there both for horse stealing and for murder. He had been arrested and jailed for the crimes but, following the custom of the day, relatives had 'made bond' and freed him in order to let him flee the country to avoid standing trial. He was the earlier version of the modern 'remittance' man; paid a monthly remittance by relatives to stay away from them.

'You sure about that, Bert?' he demanded, his breath reeking. 'I mean about them hiring men to fight the sheepmen? If that's true, I reckon I'll just go up. I'll fight sheep any time, and it won't be the first time I've killed a

31

man,' he added boastingly.

The man Bert shrugged and waited for Tony to bring the cut plug tobacco. He was a peaceful, stolid, steady-working cowpuncher who had asked the question only because of the hunger for news of the outside world that loneliness brings.

But all of them there that day knew that the war already brewed was beginning to boil, and while they were confident that there would be no repercussions this far south, there was in every one of them, with the possible exception of Joe Beckum, the secret fear that the war might spread.

Johnathan Breuger, the Colorado German sheep baron who grazed two hundred and sixty thousand head of 'woolies,' as the cowmen called them, was rich almost beyond imagination. He was rich because each year his ewes produced one hundred percent profit from their lambs and their wool. The wool paid expenses and in the fall the full grown fat lambs were worth more untold thousands of dollars in the multi-millionaire German's already bulging money sacks. He had paid money to the right men in the Capitol at Washington and they had assured him he was within the law in driving south into what ten years ago had been almost solidly controlled Apache country.

The cowmen, on the other hand, were mostly money poor, no matter how many head they grazed. They hated Halliburton and his herders because of secret envy at the huge profits being made, they hated them bitterly because their grass was turning into gold in the German sheep baron's coffers, and they hated sheep because they grazed the already poor range down to the roots and waxed fat where cows would starve. Their sharp hooves, moreover, cut deep trails by the thousands down into the grass roots, and left the hard-driving spring rains to come along and complete the job of erosion, leaving land that never again would grow grass.

The year before, the year Geronimo had surrendered, Breuger, having been assured from Washington that he was within his rights, drove the first big bands comprising ten thousand head onto ranges that cowmen had long considered to be their own by the pioneer right of possession, long before the Apaches were put on reservations. There hadn't been much actual opposition except for a few sporadic outbursts of gunfire from long range that did no damage except to kill a few 'woolies.' That and a cold warning from old Lem Cooley to Halliburton that he'd darned well better get the hell and gone off Cooley's grass, because he didn't want the smelly woolies ruining his vast ranges and stinking up water-holes to the point where the cows wouldn't drink.

Sam Halliburton, a fearless, hard-bitten, quiet-eyed man of forty, had listened quietly while the stolid-faced, Winchester-carrying herders imported from Chihuahua as both herders and fighters waited for the shooting to start. Halliburton paid no heed to the warning and went on moving the two bands of five thousand each to where the best grass and water could be found. That fall he drove his ewes and the rolypoly lambs, now as large as their mothers, back to Colorado to winter feeding grounds, taking with him Lem Cooley's words.

Breuger's answer, this second year, was ninety thousand head back over the Mogollon rim with two words to Halliburton, 'Feed them.'

It was then that Lem Cooley went into action.

CHAPTER FOUR

He was eating dinner that day in a dining room on a hard-packed, dirty floor; a monster room in a monster building that was almost a castle. The west and south walls of the house were forty feet above the ground, with stairs leading up over the *ramada* to a round, shoulder-high enclosure on top. It was from this that old man Burton had shot the first of the Apache raiders that morning in the long ago. The rest of the ranch buildings themselves formed an enclosure one hundred yards square, with a well inside in case of siege. This Cooley had built to stay.

And during the Civil War, when all but a mere handful of troops had been called east into the fighting, Cochise the deadly Chiricahua leader, collaborating with the Tontos and Warm Springs and Jicarillas and Mescaleros and others of Apacheria—Cochise drove the settlers from their ranches and homesteads to the safety of either the walled city of old Tucson or into smaller pioneer towns such as Wilcox.

All except two. Pete Kichin in his fortress a few miles north of where Nogales now stands, and Lem Cooley in his fortress up near Feather Creek in Apache Basin.

Thus that day at noon when the rider came loping into the enclosure on a sweating horse and hurried inside with the news that the Mogollon rim was white with sheep, Lem Cooley let out one of his roaring oaths and got up from the long table.

He stood there wiping his meat-greasy hands on his thighs and then across his tobacco-stained white beard. His grey hair hung down past his ears in ringlets unwashed for years. The eyes that stared back at the buck-toothed rider were bright, strangely bright.

'So they came back ag'in this year after I warned 'em not to, hey?'

'That's about the size of it, Lem,' Ron Parker, the Texan, replied.

He was about twenty-eight, very tall and angular; another who had found it expedient to leave his native state or go to the penitentiary. He affected a long yellow mustache that hid his mouth and twitched when he grinned the fishy-eyed grin now in evidence.

'Where's your cousin, Pete?' Cooley demanded suspiciously. He knew Pete only too well. Good for fighting pay, but a glutton for liquor.

Parker was reaching for a slab of roast meat on the rough board table. He said, 'He's in San Marino, Lem.'

'Why'n Hades ain't he up there at the lookout camp where he's supposed to be?' roared the rancher angrily. 'What does the lazy Texas son think that I pay him fer?'

Parker chewed, gulped, and wiped at his

mouth. He stood there with the meat in his hands and grinned at their employer. 'Wal, you know Pete, Lem. He's a restless cuss and he didn't take much to stayin' up there day after day, just sittin' on his behind under a tree with a pair of field glasses. So he told me he was goin' down to San Marino settlement and git us a few bottles of whiskey to sort of break up the monotony.'

'Yeah? And when was this?'

Parker said, 'Uh, two or three days ago.'

'You mean two or three weeks ago,' the old man almost snarled at him. 'Now you stop stuffin' yer gut with that meat long enough to listen to me, hear me? As soon as you git full you get on a fresh hoss and burn the breeze to San Marino after that no account cousin of yourn and tell him to get the hell and gone back up there and start earnin' the fighting wages I'm payin' you two pups, hear me? You came in here lookin' fer fightin' pay because yo're both too lazy to work, and by goddlemighty yo're goin to earn it, hear me?'

Parker nodded and used his yellow teeth to tear at another bite of the roast. He didn't tell the angry old man with the long hair that he actually had left camp the day before and ridden to the settlement; that he had found Pete, whose name also was Parker and who looked more like a brother than a cousin, in an adobe shack with a Mexican woman whose husband had deserted her; that Pete had, temporarily at least, lost interest in a grass war.

He said, 'Why, shore, I'll tell him, Lem. What do you want us to do? How you want us to go about it?'

'You'll do exactly what I tell you, hear me? You git Pete and move in on one of them bands. Take yer time an' don't let 'em see you, meanin' keep off the skyline. When you git things lined up on one of them bands an' can do it without bein' seen, kill the herders an' leave 'em lay. Burn their camp. If there's any bluff handy, run as many sheep over as you can, but all of it on the quiet. Then fade out an' see that yer tracks cain't be followed. Go back to yer camp an' wait fer me. I'll be up in about a week to look things over. If ye've done a good job ye git paid.'

'Fifty apiece fer them two or three herders, eh? What you promised?'

'You'll git yer money,' snapped back the old man. 'Now fill yerself with gut waddin' an't git out of here an' back up there to work.'

He turned and stomped out into trash-littered dirt beneath the long *ramada* of brush, kicked a sleeping hound yelpingly out of the way, bit at a plug of black tobacco, and strode off. Parker ate his fill, got up and slapped a fat

Mexican woman on her broad arm, and went out to his tired horse. He'd spurred it unmercifully to make his trip look good. He led the animal fifty yards across the compound and between two sheds, then through an archway in the forty-foot wall big enough for the passage of a huge freight wagon. Here were the corrals, built close by the walls for the gunfire protection of horses and mules when the Apaches struck.

Parker roped and saddled a big chestnut, swung up, and loped away to the north to make it look good to the hawk eyes that he knew were watching him. He was chuckling to himself and feeling very, very cunning. He was not going to San Marino for Pete, and the chuckles were in anticipation of Pete's futile roars of rage when he found out that love had deprived him of fifty dollars.

He made the thirty-mile trip by sundown and rode into a draw where a thin trickle of water from the spring, and the choked brush on both sides, made an ideal hidden camp. By climbing the ridge on the west side to a cluster of rocks, he could sit beneath the trees up there and see the green panorama for miles in all directions. He hunted up the hobbled pack horse, unhobbled and led it back to camp and unsaddled the sweaty chestnut. By the time darkness came down Ron Parker had eaten, and carefully cleaned both his .30–30 Winchester repeater and his Colt .45 six-shooter.

Daylight found him wide awake and impatiently hurrying breakfast in order to be on his way, a strange, eager excitement firing him with an inner glow. He thought to himself with much self-satisfaction: This is the kind of work a real man is cut out for. When the chips are down and there's a tough job to do, they allus call in us Texans because we're fightin' men. We don't run and we don't back down, because we got the kind of guts these Arizona cowmen ain't got. All except old Lem. He shoulda been born down where we was—or maybe the salty old son of a rancher was, I'll ast him next time I see him.

By the time the sun was up he gigged up out of the brush-choked draw with its hidden camp and turned southward, impatient and yet taking his time because he had plenty of it and he wanted to do a perfect job. He was a little disappointed that Cooley had said to kill only the two or three herders with one band. He consoled himself that the sheepmen wouldn't quit and that there would be ample, lucrative work in the months to come. There was no fear of the law, because Cooley had snorted contemptuously at the mention of it. He'd said that he'd told the sheriff at San

40

Marino, who was only a blasted Mexican anyhow, that he'd better keep out of the way if any fighting started.

And now it was starting, Parker thought that morning.

He tugged at the lead rope of the pack horse and rode on up to the next ridge.

For days he bided his time, watching with the glasses from high vantage points. The valley that lay spread out below him was thirty miles long and seven miles wide, the best of Cooley's winter range. Here in the old days the Apaches had killed a few of his cattle for beef, but not many, because ammunition was scarce and must be hoarded, and arrows were hard to make. From where he sat Parker could see four of the great bands of five thousand head each spread out in different parts of the vast panorama, the very heart blood of Lem Cooley's best range; two men and eight sheep dogs to a band, with a burro to carry their water kegs, light blanket rolls, and the supplies brought in by busy packers. Four bands that from the heights where Parker watched that particular morning looked like four white handkerchiefs spread out on the grass to dry.

Parker bided his time and waited, and then one afternoon the opportunity he had been seeking came. The five thousand head of woolies were grazing in a half-mile-long stream of moving white along the base of a gentle declivity where cattle once had foraged. Now they were down in the more sparse section of the land because of polluted water and because men with guns were killing them at every opportunity, both for beef and for spite. It was rather late in the afternoon, and the two herders, sitting on rocks from which they could look down upon the band, were grazing them back to the place where they were temporarily camped as long as the grass held out. Out on the fringes of the band, six of the well-trained dogs kept their allotted places. If a small group started to move off, a shout in Spanish from one of the black-bearded men from Chihuahua would send a fleet-footed dog to turn back the bunch quitters.

Parker, his two horses tied out of sight back in the brush, inched forward on his belly a little closer, weighed the chances of being seen by a sharp-eyed sheep dog, and knew that the big moment he'd been waiting so impatiently for had come.

He rested his elbows in the grass, took careful aim, and gently squeezed the trigger.

CHAPTER FIVE

He shot the herder on the left squarely through the back at a distance of not more than fifty yards and knew as the man tumbled off the rock that his aim had been perfect and therefore deadly. The dead man's body hardly had struck when he jacked out the empty shell and took aim at the second man whirling to grab for his rifle. It was so close and easy that the Texan almost lazily lined the sights on the frantically moving second man, watched him drop in a limp heap with the high-pitched report of the rifle.

Parker jumped to his feet, rifle ready, and then began a cautious walk forward, watching for signs of movement beyond the rocks. Nothing came, and finally he relaxed, let down the hammer on the .30–30, and stood there with it dangling in one hand while he looked down at the two victims. They were both stone dead, killed instantly by the heart-piercing bullets; hairy-faced, tough-looking men who also had drawn fighting pay if it was necessary to fight.

'Maybe,' Parker spoke aloud and grinned through his yellowish mustache, 'this might be a hint to them others that maybe they ought to go back home where men ain't so tough.'

Still grinning, he pulled his six-shooter and shot both men through the head, knowing how much rage there would be, along with a little fear too perhaps, when the other Mexicans found out. He thought, Well, that's what Lem wanted, by crackey.

He moved leisurely back up the incline, reloading as he went, chocked the repeater into its boot and swung up, leaving the pack horse. He jogged down past the two lax bodies, then changed his mind and dismounted. He had forgotten to smash the stocks of their rifles. This the killer did, while an uneasily whining and barking sheep dog shied around like a circling coyote. Those dogs had been raised with Mexicans and among sheep, and recognized no strangers.

Mounting again, Lem Cooley's hired killer loped down through the center of the band, scattering them right and left; regretful that the terrain did not allow for a stampede over a good high bluff. That would come later. He thought grinningly, It kinda looks like this is goin' to be a right profitable summer.

He loped up and reined his horse in front of their crude camp, looking about him and then cursing at sight of the green cowhide thrown carelessly aside. It wasn't much of a camp, because these men were perfectly at home anywhere in the wilderness, with as few conveniences as the Apaches that once had claimed this land.

Just two bed-rolls, called *mochilas*, a few simple cooking utensils near two fire-blackened rocks, a packsaddle for the burro, one big wooden water keg, small portions of simple staples such as flour, beans, coffee. That was all.

Parker swung down and set fire to a large pile of dry brush they had gathered for their cooking fires. Into it he tossed everything: bed-rolls, packsaddles, and then the food.

'I reckon when them other herders git here seems like they'd oughta thank me for havin' a meal all cooked fer 'em,' he chuckled, pleased at his own wit.

The burro that carried their simple belongings was grazing hobbled a hundred yards away, and the killer's first shot sent it down kicking. He put two more bullets into it for good measure. One of the sheep dogs was baying him now, and a final shot stopped that. Parker grinned again as he dragged the limp carcass over near the fire and left it.

Nothing in the world could so enrage sheepmen as the killing of a good well-trained, loyal sheep dog.

With a final burst of .45 bullets through the

wooden water keg, Ron Parker loped away from the ruins of the camp, feeling much satisfaction at a job well done and an easily earned one hundred dollars.

Pete, he grinned to himself, was going to be a mighty mad and disgusted man.

Pete's cousin scattered the sheep again as he loped through on his way back to the pack horse. He led off toward the northwest, hunting for the rocky places, cutting a long circle before heading back directly to the hidden camp. He covered more than twenty miles before darkness forced a halt. Then he made a fireless camp, though he was many miles away from the eighteen great bands and Halliburton's supply camp headquarters. Daylight found him again on the way, and he covered about twenty-five more miles until, shortly before noon, he topped a ridge above the familiar brush-choked draw and descended the other side.

But the dancing expectation in his eyes at thought of Pete turned to disappointment and then anger as he found the camp still deserted and as he'd left it. He'd been eagerly waiting to see Pete's reactions upon hearing of his cousin's single-handed exploits; but his cousin was still down in the Mexican settlement. Parker angrily unsaddled and hobbled his horses and flopped down on his tarp-covered bed-roll. He'd wait another two or three days until Cooley came up to get a first-hand report and then, if Pete didn't show up. . .

Pete Parker didn't show up, and neither did Lem Cooley, and a new kind of impatience began to take hold of the killer. He lolled about camp and made no effort to see if any more sheep were coming in. On that particular afternoon he rose from his bunk beneath a bush, scratched at his hairy face, and went up the ridge to look at a quail trap he'd made of slender sticks lashed together into a pyramid-shaped box that could be set on edge. The trigger, known as the 'Figure 4,' was made from three notched sticks so contrived that when one of the quail, feeding on some of the extra grain he had packed in for the horses, touched it, the notches fell apart and let the tilted side drop to the ground.

Parker climbed up to the lookout point and saw that the trap was down, with a number of mountain quail fluttering around inside, their little top-knots bobbing as they tried frantically to find a way out. He knelt beside the trap and began to remove the dirt from a scooped out place beneath one edge. The hand that had pulled trigger on two more men reached inside and brought out a fluttering bundle of feathers. He placed a boot over the

47

hole and was in the act of pulling off the bird's head when some instinct caused him to freeze and then turn slowly.

Twenty feet away, near the brush clump where they had been waiting, stood three men with guns at their hips. Parker's face paled beneath his whisker stubble as he recognized two of them. He'd seen Frank and Stub Burton more than once down in San Marino, drinking and making love to the Mexican girls whose language was native to the two men.

'Never mind, Parker,' Frank Burton said, moving in closer, the muzzle of the .44 steady. 'Just turn it loose.'

'Trapped, by golly!' laughed Stub. 'Trapped by a quail trap. We was hopin' you'd come up an' look at it so's we wouldn't have to wait until you went to sleep tonight.'

The killer rose to his feet and let the bird go. It burred off, bullet-like, and Frank Burton said, 'Just turn the others loose, too, Parker. You ain't goin' to have much appetite tonight anyhow.'

Parker automatically did as he was told, and the eight other free birds were gone in a flash. He straightened, and his face was still pale, something tight gripping at his vitals, cold fear in his heart.

'What's it all about, Frank?' he asked, hoping that by some kind of a heaven-sent miracle either Pete or Lem Cooley would show up and show up in a hurry.

'Cut it out,' Stub Burton laughed. 'You didn't think you could get away with it, now did you, mister?'

'I don't know what you're talkin' about.'

'Tie his hands behind him, Bud,' the older Burton directed a sloping-shouldered man of about twenty-six. This narrow-bodied man was another of the 'warriors' who had come into the country seeking fighting pay. Parker stood rigidly while Bud Tracy thonged his wrists with piggin string. He could feel the man's hands trembling, and that fact in itself told him what to expect. They had not shot him as he lay on his bed-roll. They had waited to take him alive.

And there was only *one* reason why.

They were going to hang him.

CHAPTER SIX

Bud Tracey stepped back, the prominent Adam's apple in his stringy throat bobbing up and down as he swallowed convulsively. Never a very bright man, and certainly not a strong one because of his amazingly narrow shoulders, his ambitions had run mostly to

49

being known as a bad man to tangle with. He had been firmly convinced in his own mind that he had more cold nerve than any other man alive. He had said to Halliburton, as the group of men looked down at the two crumpled figures under swarms of flies:

'Mister Halliburton, I kin trail a lizard acrost a hot rock, an' I give ye my word, I'll find the gent who did this an' we'll string him up.'

Halliburton's hard, business-like eyes bored at him with cool contempt as he snapped, 'That's why you're getting paid.' He turned to Frank Burton. 'Have any idea who it might have been?'

'No telling,' Frank replied. 'Some of them no-account Texans in big hats who work for old Cooley. Used to be a lot of them around when me an' Stub was kids on the ranch; all of them out here for their health. I've seen a lot of them hanging around them Mexican girls over at San Marino.'

'Think you can trail him?'

'I reckon we can.'

Halliburton turned, stiffened a leg to ease his seat in the saddle and spoke to the Mexican packer who had discovered the bodies the day after the murders and made a hard run to the main camp to break the news. He spoke in Spanish.

'Have those herders get busy on a grave and bury these men, and then get out there and round up those sheep. They're scattered for four miles.'

He reached into a pocket and brought out a sheaf of greenbacks and began to count off. Once he looked up and let his hard gaze burn into the faces of the three waiting men. 'I'm paying you two hundred and fifty apiece to keep on the trail of the man who did this and then hang him. You understand? I said *hang* him. If you double-cross me and run out on the job, you'd better keep right on going and never come back, because no man yet has ever done that to me and got away with it. That clear?'

'You needn't worry,' Frank said. 'We'll take care of it.'

'Good. Here's your money. As soon as you get him or maybe there were two of them, since there were two horses—you burn the breeze out of this country and lay low for about two months. If Lem Cooley is still alive by then, come on back and I might have some more work for you. Lay low and keep your mouths shut, and if you get drunk and start talking too much I'll not only deny it but I'll stop your mouths for good. Here.'

He handed them the money and returned the rest of it to a hip pocket. The four silent

51

herders he had brought with him from the main camp were coming down the slope with a pick and shovels. Halliburton reined around to return to his tent camp headquarters fifteen miles away.

'Get goin',' he ordered, and turned his back upon them without waiting for a reply.

That was when the bragging had begun, while the three men followed at a snail's pace the trail left by two horses, sometimes working on foot among the rocks. And now Bud Tracy was standing there with his hands trembling and his prominent Adam's apple bobbing up and down, and he was beginning to get sick in his stomach.

'Wha—what do we do now, Frank?' He swallowed, and licked nervously at his dry lips.

'Look at him!' jeered Stub, and laughed. 'He's plumb green around the gills.'

Frank Burton stepped in front of the doomed man and looked at him out of a pair of coal black eyes. 'Where's that cousin Pete of yourn?' he asked.

'He ain't here. He's been gone fer two or three weeks,' Parker said in a low voice.

'You're lying!' replied Frank harshly. 'There was two hosses tied up there in the brush above where you shot them two herders off the rocks. Two empty .30–30 shells fifty yards away.'

'I tell you he wasn't with me,' insisted the killer doggedly. 'That was my pack hoss. You didn't think I'd be ridin' around with no grub or anything?'

'Well, anyhow,' Stub said in satisfaction, 'the blasted sidewinder admits that he done it. We gonna string him up now, Frank?'

'No,' Frank said, shaking his head. 'We'll go down and cook him a good supper and stay on guard tonight to see if Pete comes in. If he does, we'll just make shore there won't be any danger of gettin' shot in the back later on when we come back here.'

They took Parker down below and remained with him through the night, two of them sleeping while a third remained on guard. But when daylight came and the hoped for man had not arrived, Frank Burton ordered breakfast fixed and the horses saddled. Parker's mustached lips were tight as they walked him up the slope to the lookout tree. He didn't speak until they shoved him beneath a limb about ten feet above the ground. Then his iron nerve broke.

'Look,' he pleaded. 'We're all in this together, just on different sides, that's all. We ain't mad at each other. If you'll let me go I'll git outa the country—'

'Shut up,' Stub said. 'You'd double-cross

53

your own grandmother, like all the rest of the Big-Hats.'

'I swear I wouldn't!'

'Like fun you wouldn't,' sneered Frank.

'How come you hate me?' pleaded the doomed killer. 'I never done nothin' to you.'

'The devil you didn't!' snarled Stub, his black eyes burning with sudden anger. 'When you had old Lem's Big-Hats behind you, you called us a couple of blamed greasers, didn't you? Said that down in Texas they kill a Mexican like they kill a rattlesnake, didn't you? You said all that, but you shore didn't show it around them Mexican girls at San Marino, did you? You shot a couple of 'greasers' in the back and then beg two more of us 'greasers' to turn you loose. I ought to smash in yore dirty, stinking face!'

Frank stepped in and pushed his younger brother back. He said, 'None of that, kid. We'll do our squaring up another and better way.' And to Tracy: 'Get your rope and hurry it up. Let's get finished and get out of here. The bigger head start we get, the better. Should have done it last night.'

But Tracy came back with the coiled manila in his hands and then stood there in helpless uncertainty, swallowing hard and seemingly unsure of his next move.

'Don't stand there,' snapped Frank at him.

'Throw it over that limb and slip the loop over his head. Pull that knot up under his left ear. Might as well,' he said with brittle humor, 'send him out in style like the regular sheriffs do.'

Stub, his sudden anger vanished, began to laugh, jerking his head toward Bud Tracy. 'Boy, look at him!' he jeered. 'He was the trailin' fool who wasn't afeered of nothin', wasn't you, Bud? He blowed fer days about what he was a-goin' to do, an' now he's about blowed up.'

Tracy's long-fingered, trembling hands finally got the loop knot in position beneath Parker's left ear. The doomed man said nothing. He had regained his composure now. Flashing through his mind were a lot of things that had happened in the past: recollection of the men he had killed, some with rifle shots in the back from ambush.

He had been a hard, callous, brutal man, spawned in the backwash of a generation that had killed for four years and then come home to kill again. He had picked up where they had left off, hiring his guns to Lem Cooley for a price in a ruthless war where many men would be doomed to die. Some kind of an inescapable fate had decreed that he should kill the first two and then himself be the third to die.

These were the last thoughts of the man far from home country as three Arizonians in leather shotgun chaps gripped work-hardened fingers around the rope and gave a mighty heave. Parker's booted feet swept off the ground and his body began to spin slowly. The three ran the free end of the rope around the trunk of the big pine and tied it securely.

Stub stepped back, removed his hat, and wiped at his forehead. 'He's sure a heavy son of a gun,' he said, watching the spinning body and the legs that were drawing themselves up and down convulsively. Parker's face was turning black, his tongue protruding, and there was froth on his lips. But Tracy turned around with a queer, strangled sound, and the contents of his breakfast spilled out on the ground. He staggered over to a boulder and leaned on it for support, while the sweat broke out on his forehead and his knees shook.

'Goddlemighty!' he whimpered, and then he broke down. He sat down on the ground and placed his horse face with the buck teeth down between his knees and began to bawl, his skinny shoulders shaking convulsively. 'Oh, goddlemighty!'

Stub Burton looked at his older brother and jerked a thumb suggestively. 'You'd think,' he complained, 'that he'd got lost in the herd and cain't find his maw.'

Frank bent and got the man by the shoulder and shook him roughly. 'Get up on your feet,' he ordered, 'and stop that silly bellerin'. You wanted in on this, and you got what you wanted.'

Tracy staggered to his feet and stood there wiping at his eyes and mouth with the bandana that sagged at his skinny throat. He had his back to the slowly spinning figure hanging by its neck.

'We don't know what yo're goin' to do,' Frank said, 'but we sure as shootin' don't want you with us. Where you goin'?'

Bud Tracy swallowed and wiped at his eyes again. 'I'm hittin' fer Colorady jest as fast as I kin git there. I've had all this cattle war I want. Him just a-hangin' there kickin'—'

'Shut up! I told you you asked for it. All right, you better get rolling, and if you get caught you'd better keep yore mouth shut unless you want to do a little kickin' on yore own. All right, kid; let's get rolling. It's a long ways to Stinking Springs.'

They went to their horses and mounted. There were no goodbyes. The three men fell away in three different directions. The last sound of a hoof clattering over rocks died away, and silence came to the place where that object was no longer turning.

It hung motionless.

57

CHAPTER SEVEN

As for old Lem Cooley, he came out of the
fortress-like house that morning onto the
trash-littered earth beneath the *ramada*,
crossed the compound to the big archway in
the wall and strode over to where a Mexican
youth of sixteen was waiting. He placed the
food his Mexican wife had fixed for him in the
two saddle bags and rode away from the ranch
at a good clip, grim satisfaction in his fierce
old soul. A rider had come by the day before
with news that two Mexican sheepherders had
been found dead, shot in the back; first grim
warning to Johnathan Breuger that if he
wanted to graze his sheep on Cooley's vast
domain the price would have to be paid in
blood. He set a course for San Marino twelve
miles away and made the chinless roan horse
with the blue legs earn its feed; chewing the
black tobacco and spitting into the wind and
wiping at his dark-streaked beard. He made
the twelve miles in two hours, dropping down
the slope into a narrow valley cut through by a
creek now dry; the land on each side was
dotted by adobe huts and green fields of foot-
high corn, some cotton, vegetables, and here
and there small orchards.

The roan slobbered and blew as it plodded through the deep sand of the wagon road to the other side of the creek. Cooley gigged it up the opposite bank and then loped down what passed for a street before a long line of adobe houses built wall to wall. At a corner he swung in between two buildings and then cut over to a tree-shaded house much larger than the others. A sign above the porch read, *Jesus Dominguez, Sheriff.*

'Hey, Jesus!' roared the old man. 'Come out of there, blast you, if you're still not in bed yet.'

Cooley didn't deign to get down. He sat there as the front door opened and a big, well-fed-looking Mexican wearing a white shirt and corduroys and shiny black boots came out onto the porch. He had a napkin around his neck.

'Hello, Lem,' the sheriff greeted him. 'W'at bring you over here to my humble house?'

Cooley snorted and spat past the roan's left shoulder and wiped at his dirty beard. He knew that Dominguez was a good enough sheriff to hold the preponderantly Mexican population in check, and he held the usual Anglo's contempt for him.

'You know very well what brought me over here,' snapped the old man. 'A rider come by yesterday and says as how there's been a

59

couple of them Chihuahua woolie herders got kilt. I just come by to tell ye that I didn't have nothin' to do with it, so ye better not start nosin' around, sabe?'

'Sure, I know, Meester Cooley. I don't think you dawn it.'

'Me an' none of my men neither.'

'I know one who don' dawn it,' the sheriff said uncomfortably. 'Meester Cooley, I wish you make him go home. I no want to make trouble, because he work for you. But this woman she like him, an' he been with her t'ree-four weeks now, and now her husband come back but she don't wanta go with him no more. So he come to me and ask me to go make him go away. But Pete say if I don't shud up he gonna—'

'Pete!' roared Cooley, his face beneath the beard becoming apoplectic with rage. 'Pete Parker?'

'Si, Pedro. He been here all the time dronk—'

'Where is he?' bellowed Cooley.

The sheriff pointed to an adobe cabin down the lane about two hundred yards distant. 'Down there. I wish you go—'

But Cooley already had gone. He jerked the roan's head over hard and slashed the ends of the reins down across its flanks and spurred at a run toward the cabin. He hauled up hard

60

and swung down and strode through the open door where a Mexican woman was at work on a rock stove in a corner, and in another corner a man lay sprawled asleep on a pallet. Cooley let out a roar and drew back his boot, cursing and kicking while the frightened woman fled out the back door.

'You dirty wuthless pup!' snarled the old man, grabbing him by an arm and dragging him out onto the dirt floor. 'Workin' fer me, hey? Watching them woolies, was ye? I'll show ye!'

Pete Parker finally came alive enough to ward off the blows and instinctively slugged back. He knocked Cooley into a wall and stood glowering, his eyes blood-shot.

'Git on yer clothes an' git saddled,' the old man snarled at him. 'Fer two cents I'd bust yer head open with a gun barrel. Git dressed. There's trouble with the woolie men.'

Fifteen minutes later the two loped away from the settlement and headed for the higher country, pushing the horses hard as though they already knew what had happened. And any doubts about it were erased when at noon they sat their horses and looked at the motionless figure hanging from the limb.

Pete Parker, looking much as the dead man had, passed a hand across his reddish bloated face. He said nothing, but swung down and went to the knotted rope, while Cooley's sharp old eyes were scanning the ground. He began to ride in circles and finally found one set of tracks that led north. He followed these for half a mile, came back and picked up the second trail, then the third. By the time he finished Pete had scratched out a shallow grave with the hammer of the dead man's six-shooter, buried him, and then covered the mound with large sized rocks.

'Three of 'em,' Cooley announced, and leaned his bony back against the tree trunk where, shortly before, a rope had been knotted around it. 'One went north, meanin' that he probably wasn't from around here. I'll put Casey an' an Apache trailer after him. The other two went southwest and southeast. You go after one and I'll go after the other.'

Pete Parker lifted his bloodshot eyes to the fierce old man's grey-bearded face. He hadn't eaten in two days and the long ride had shaken his tortured nerves and left him weak.

'We'll get them,' he said in a strangely quiet voice. 'Then I'm coming back here and go after Halliburton. *I'm going to hang him just like he hung my cousin.*'

'Well, ye won't by standin' around talkin' about it. Git on yer horse an' take that trail headin' southwest. I'll take the other one. I've already found the hosses an' unhobbled 'em.

They'll find their way back to the ranch. I'll have ter break off long enough to go ter the ranch an' leave orders about what to do while I'm gone, an' have Casey hit thet trail headin' north. Come on.'

They left Ron Parker's bed-roll and few personal belongings to the destroying hand of the elements and rode away, Lem Cooley unaware that his brutal spilling of blood, instead of electing to resort to the courts to settle his grievances against the sheep interests, was to affect the lives of many people far to the south; peaceful people who held no grievances, had no grudges to settle, wanted only the opportunity to work out their destinies without fear or hatred.

Nor would the old Indian killer have cared had he known.

For him there was only one code: his own. Take what you wanted by force, hold it by force, and kill ruthlessly those who barred the way.

CHAPTER EIGHT

In Tony Brown's place that afternoon, Joe Beckum was still blustering about the sheep invasion of Arizona by the Colorado baron, to the point where the man Bert finally went back into the kitchen to eat a couple of the *Señora's* good *tacos* and drink a cup of her strong black coffee. She still had the pretty face of the girl of six years before, but her body had become buxom now, and there were two boys playing around on the hard-packed dirt floor.

'It's like I tell you, Tony,' Beckum continued loudly. 'The way I figger it, if we don't stop them up there, it won't be no time at all till they'll be down here to eat up what little grazin' these desert cowmen get, which is little enough. . .'

Tony left him and carried a bottle of tequila over to serve four men sitting around a rude table. Samuel Ernest leaned lazily on the end of the bar, his back to Beckum who, having no audience, returned to his own table. One of the four looked at the former minister and grinned. They long since had ceased to offer him drinks and banter with him about his religion, respecting him for his beliefs, admiring him for his good common sense in not preaching to them about the evils of drinking and cursing.

'What do you think of all this business, Parson?' a man at the table asked.

A slow smile crossed the gentle features of the man from the East. 'Why, Tom, you boys already know that there is only one way that a man of my former calling can feel. One of the Ten Commandments is, 'Thou Shalt Not Kill.' God breathed life into man's body after giving him that body to keep that spark of life going, to house the soul until time for it to leave. You know something, Tom? I was down along the water's edge near the Hangman's Tree the other day, lazing in the sun on the bank, and right near me was an old rotted cottonwood limb covered with a kind of fungus or moss. In one of the cracks in that rotting log I saw a larva of some kind inside a cocoon. While I sat there watching, I saw life emerge from the cocoon and watched a beautiful insect that looked like a dragon fly emerge slowly and crawl out into the warm sun. For two or three minutes it remained there while its wet wings unfolded slowly and began to dry. Then it took flight, rising higher in the air, and flew away into the unknown, leaving behind a lifeless shell. That, Tom, is my conception of man's life here upon earth. When he dies his soul takes flight; proving, I believe, that life in all forms is exactly the same.'

Beckum sneered and put down his empty glass. 'What's that got to do with shootin' a blasted Mexican sheepherder?' he demanded dourly.

Ernest flicked a glance at Tony, received a slight shrug in return. He said patiently, 'God prepared man's soul inside his body as he prepared that beautiful thing that flew from the cocoon. When the soul leaves the body it takes flight. But when Man steps in and destroys, he is destroying his own soul, which is God's handiwork. I remember when those men caught and you helped hang that young fellow whom I buried—'

'He was a hoss thief!' snapped out Beckum, conveniently forgetting in the heat of the argument that he himself was wanted back in San Saba County, Texas, for the same offense. 'Maybe the man he stole that hoss from was left on foot and died because of it, an inch at a time, while the thief who done it kept ridin' along fine. Meanin' that he got what was comin' to him and that the country is better off because we hung him. I suppose yo're goin' to say that because I helped I'm goin' to remain right here in this 'dobie cocoon. Haw-haw-haw!' he roared gleefully. 'That's a good 'un, that'n is.' He choked off his laughter and snorted. 'Gimme another drink, Tony. "Destroyin' God's handiwork," he says. Pah!'

Ernest made no reply but turned at the sound of a horse in front of the building. There came a jangle of spur rowels; then a shadow darkened the doorway and a young

66

rider came in. He was not yet at the age of maturity, as evidenced by the faint line on his upper lip indicating a valiant effort to grow a mustache. He wore a roll-brim, high-crowned Mexican 'Chihuahua' hat, short leather *chaparajas* that came to just below the knees, two-inch spur rowels, and the inevitable pistol at his right hip.

He strode in with all the brashness and confidence of youth and leaned against the short bar, surveying the others with bland insouciance.

'Howdy,' he greeted Tony. 'Ain't been by here in a couple of years. Got anything to cut the alkali out of a man's throat?'

Tony suppressed a smile at the word 'man' and picked up a bottle of mescal. 'This be all right?'

'Just right.'

Tony poured, and the brash youngster picked up the glass and tossed it off without benefit of water. 'Just fill it again,' he said without batting an eye.

He picked up the second glass and eyed it speculatively. 'Mescal, the national drink of Mexico ... along with tequila and pulque. Border only thirty miles away and nobody to stop the smugglers. No offense.' He laughed at Tony's slight frown. 'I sent a message a couple of weeks ago by one of them heading for Wilcox. Got a brother who tends bar there. He can speak Apache,' he offered, grinning.

Joe Beckum eyed the youngster sourly. He was drunk enough to be mean, still irked about the sheep situation in Apache Basin. He said, 'I don't remember you mentioning your name.'

'Nope,' was the cheerful reply. 'You don't because I didn't.'

Beckum was still eyeing him narrowly. 'I got a hunch I've seen you some place before.'

'Never heard of the place. Might have been my brother, who used to be a good outdoor man before the sun cooked his brain and he had to work in the shade. All of us brothers look alike. It was probably our father's fault,' he added apologetically.

It was obvious to the now quiet listeners that this brash, good-looking, blond-headed youngster was deliberately baiting Joe Beckum, something that caused an exchange of uneasy glances. Beckum had proven in several drunken fights that he was a bad man while under the influence of liquor. Tolerated by Tony only because he had money to spend, he was treated with brusque civility by the others because he'd jumped in and helped a posse of strangers, who themselves might have been outlaws, hang that unknown young fellow the previous summer.

'It's strange I don't remember yore name,' he persisted.

'It's not strange you don't remember what you never knew,' came the bland reply.

One of the men let go a nervous snicker and Beckum began to glower. He covered his rising anger with a cloak of sneering sarcasm.

'I presume yo're travelin,' he said bitingly.

'Go right ahead and presume just as much as you want to as long as you don't interrupt my drinking.'

More snickers, open now. The men were beginning to enjoy the surly Texan's discomfiture.

'So you been through this country before, eh?' he sneered.

'Suppose I have?'

'You must know quite a lot about it then, if you ain't been through in a couple of years.'

'I heard that sheep was sorta puttin' pore cowpunchers outa jobs,' grinned the tow-headed young drinker of the fiery mescal.

And then it *did* get quiet in the room. This was no longer a joke. The youngster had just finished his third drink and was pouring another, blandly ignoring the dead quiet of the place. A chair scraped as Joe Beckum got to his feet.

'That sounds like sheep talk to me,' he half snarled, hand hovering over his gun butt.

Bill Allen turned slowly and eyed the speaker coolly. His own hand lay close to the butt of the pistol at his hip. 'The man I work for has got several thousand of them,' he said coldly. 'Now let me tell you something, mister. Where I came from and where I'm going is my own damned business. I drink my likker straight and keep my nose in my own back yard; and you better do the same, sabe?'

He turned his back on the other in contempt and looked at Tony, indicating the bottle on the bar. 'Gimme a full one just like it an' I'll be on my way. Got to meet somebody, if the darned old son of a gun wasn't too lazy to ride down.'

He paid for the liquor with a small Mexican gold coin, collected his change, and tucked the bottle under his arm. 'Adios, gents. Glad to have met you. That is, all except one.' He grinned and went out into the sunshine to where his big red horse stood waiting; one of the best out of Don Alphonso's great herds.

'I suppose you're goin' back to yore woolie friends,' Beckum shouted after him.

'Any place you say, dearie, any place you say,' came tauntingly, followed by boyish laughter and the creak of saddle leather.

Bill Allen uncorked the bottle, waved a bland farewell, and rode off toward the west.

The former minister smiled and shook his

head condescendingly. He said to Tony, 'Young and confident that he can conquer the world. And so many of them do it, too. There are a thousand more like him, ten thousand, a hundred thousand riding the open ranges of the cattle country all the way from Mexico to the Canadian border, from the coast of California to Missouri. Young, brash, cocky. Some will dissipate that youth and energy and spend their entire lives without a change of pattern. No family, no home, no worldly goods.'

'Just like me, Parson.' The man Bert smiled from the doorway leading into the kitchen. He was munching on a *taco*, a cup of coffee in his other hand.

'It has its rewards, Bert. Others will accumulate and become rich and respected.'

'And others,' grunted Joe Beckum angrily, 'will get their fool heads shot off fer spoutin' off at the mouth too much.'

He got up and strode through the kitchen and headed toward the outdoors to relieve his anger in the open air.

CHAPTER NINE

As for cocky young Bill Allen, he rode cheerfully on westward, following a broad path beneath the cottonwoods. He was certain in his own mind that Ed would show up; his note sent by the Mexican smuggler had been intended to sting the older brother he worshipped into coming down this afternoon. Mike and Joe, the two other brothers back in San Saba County, were all right, Bill thought; good solid citizens. Mike was even a deputy sheriff, as so many ranchers often were. But they were married men with children, and he and Ed were still single. To Bill that not only made for a much stronger bond between the two, but ... why, Ed could even speak Apache!

Bill took a swig from the bottle and grinned. He'd ride on up a few miles more, and then, if he didn't meet Ed, he'd come on back and spend the night at the Alamo, and then go on to Wilcox tomorrow. But not tonight. Thought of another verbal joust with that sheep hater back there in the Alamo was too tempting to pass up. After which he'd go on in and bedevil Ed for a few days in the saloon, and then get down to the real business at hand.

Don Alphonso had a widowed niece of about twenty-seven, and she was a beauty. . .

Bill grinned and locked a leg around the horn of the silver-mounted saddle and let the great red gelding plod along at a walk.

'Good old Ed,' he said, and cocked a reflective young eye at a distant buzzard.

'Eddie, my boy, I can't figger it out. I can't understand a man who wants to get ahead bad enough to give up a respectable profession like cowpunching and such to serve swill to swizzlers.'

'I got some sense, you young jackass, that's all.'

'Huh! That calls for something to cut the taste outa my mouth and to keep me from insulting the fambly name.'

'One more and that's all·you get. It'll stunt your growth.'

'You try to stop me and I'll stunt *your* growth. When are you going to cut out this fool business and come down to Mexico where the real opportunites are?'

'I'm quite content here, Willyum. Now look here, *Señor* Guillermo Allen, you dust your shirt tail out of here and go get some sleep. I don't mind your having a few, but there's no brother of mine getting tight in Wilcox, sabe?'

'*Seguro, que si, hermano querido.*' (Sure, yes, dear brother.)

Good old Ed. Bill Allen grinned again.

He uncorked his *chaparajaed* leg from around the saddle horn and found the stirrup, the Mexican spur rowels jangling. He took another pull at the tequila bottle, and that brought forth the desire for song.

Bill Allen leaned back and sang.

Billy Venero heard them say,
In an Arizona town one day,
That a band of Apache Indians,
Were upon the trail of death.

Heard them tell of murder done,
Three men killed at Rocky Run.
'They're in danger at the cow ranch,'
Cried Billy under his breath.

'That's me,' Bill Allen told his plodding red horse gravely. 'Only all the 'Paches are on the reservation now except old Geronimo and he's in Florida. Wonder how he likes it down there? Now lessee, where wazzi?'

He continued where he had interrupted himself.

Cow ranch forty miles away
Was a little place that lay

74

In a deep and shaded valley
Of the mighty wilderness.

Half a score of homes were there,
And in one a maiden fair,
Held the heart of Billy Venero,
Billy Venero's little Bess.

'Hmmmm,' he said thoughtfully, eyeing
the level of the bottle, which was still near the
neck. 'I never knowed one named Bess. They
were mostly called Pepita, Chiquita, Panchita,
Rosita, Margarita, Carmencita, and I think,'
he added thoughtfully, 'there was one named
Maud.'
He couldn't remember where he had left off
but took up again anyhow.

Just at dusk a horse of brown,
Wet with sweat, came pounding down,
Down the little lane at the cow ranch,
And stopped at Bessie's door.

But the cowboy was asleep,
And his slumbers were so deep,
Little Bessie could not wake him,
Though she tried forevermore.

Now you've heard this story told,
By the young and by the old,

Of the fight down at the cow ranch,
The night the 'Paches came.

Of that sharp and bloody fight,
How the chief fell in the fight,
And the terror-stricken warriors
When they heard Venero's name.

He took a final drink, corked the bottle of mescal, and slid it into a leather pouch hanging from the saddle horn. He nodded yawningly, and then yawned again. The great hacienda which he had left long before daylight lay twenty miles below the line, and the fifty-mile ride, though it had not tired him much, had made demands on his still maturing body. He knotted the reins across the red horse's neck, pulled his hat down over his eyes, and before he had gone a hundred yards more young Bill Allen was sound asleep.

As long as the horse continued its slow rocking motion Bill Allen slept the healthful sleep of the young. But presently the animal stopped, and Bill opened his eyes, yawning, and pushed back his sombrero. He saw two saddle horses, yawned again sleepily, and a voice said harshly, 'Get down off that hoss!'

He swung his gaze to the other side, and what he saw dissipated the sleep from his brain in a hurry. Standing ten feet away were two swarthy-skinned, bearded men, eyeing him from back of leveled Winchesters. Both of them were stark naked, wet, and covered with sand.

'Well, whaddaya know?' Bill Allen marveled, staring down. 'Apaches! Two rip-snortin' young bucks off the reservation on a raidin' spree. Don't you know the soldiers will be out after you?' he reproved them. 'Which one of you is Geronimo?'

'Funny feller, huh?' snarled the shorter of the two, and took a step forward, rifle all the way to his shoulder. 'Get down off that hoss!'

'Sorry,' was the apologetic reply. 'I don't savvy Apache. You'll have to wait till my brother gets here. He'll be along any minute. You savvy the sign language?' he asked, Like this?' And he stuck his thumb to his nose, twirling his fingers suggestively.

The shorter and younger of the two twisted his head aside and looked at the other. 'Say the word, Frank, and I'll shoot him out of the saddle.'

The other shook his head and stepped forward. 'Where'd you come from?' he demanded.

'The other direction from where I'm going,' Bill replied cautiously.

'It's your last chance, mister. You can step down or you kin tumble down.'

'It's all right, I won't hurt you,' Bill replied soothingly, and forthwith obeyed, grinning. He surveyed the horses and the trees with a critical eye. 'Nice ranch you got here. Good buildings and corrals and plenty of cattle. You need a new hand? I'm looking for a job.'

He reached up and removed the bottle of mescal from the pouch and, ignoring them, tilted it and took a small drink. He looked at the other two, who appeared to be a little puzzled, as though this brashness were a thing foreign to their experience.

'Well,' he said, 'I ain't goin' to beg you to drink it.'

Ten minutes later the three of them sat cross-legged in the sand, the bottle in the center, roaring with laughter over the incident.

CHAPTER TEN

Stub Burton stretched out full length on his left side, an elbow propping his head up out of the sand. He was smoking a brown paper cigarette, wet and flat between two dark fingers.

'You coulda knocked me over with a prairie dog's tail when I seen you a-comin' along

78

under the cottonwoods,' he chuckled, letting it slip off into a giggle. 'We thought you was some Mexican from down below the border. Frank an' me was cooling off in the water when we seen thet the hosses had spotted somethin'. We didn't know who to expect, an' we couldn't take any chances because ... well, just because. We was all set to start throwin' lead until we seen you rocking along in the saddle, sound asleep an' snoring.'

He went off into gales of laughter and Bill, his sombrero on the ground beside him grinned right back.

'You ain't got nothing on me, *compadre*. How do you gents think that *I* felt when I woke up and saw two fellers naked as jaybirds pointing a couple of lead sprayers at the fourth button of my shirt tail, counting up from the bottom button?'

When the laughter had died down again Frank Burton replaced the bottle in the sand. He said, 'You don't have to tell us your name if you don't want to.'

'Shucks, no reason why not. I'm Bill Allen. I live down in Mexico on the hacienda of Don Alphonso Perez y Estrada. I'm going to marry his youngest girl this fall.'

'Holy smokes!' Stub half gasped out. 'Oh, brother! old Don Alphonso. I've heard about that place.'

Bill said seriously, 'Yes, it's quite a place. There's about three hundred people on the main ranch where the Don has his headquarters. It's got its own church, where the priest is teaching me catechisms so that we can make everything all right according to their way of life.'

Frank nodded, also serious. 'We know what you mean, Bill. Our mother was a Mexican, our old man a *norteamericano*. But tell us some more about down there. You see, we're heading down that way and we might be able to get a job riding for him.'

'Easy. I'll give you a note to him. He's one Spaniard who don't hate the gringos. He ships several thousand head of cattle through Wilcox every year, and they like him up there. That's where my brother Ed is.'

He didn't see the sharp exchange of glances between the two other men, because he had taken a small drink of mescal and was picking up Stub's canteen. He drank, capped it, and went on:

'Anyhow, the old Don is running around forty-five thousand head of cattle on ranches all over Sonora and Chihuahua. He's got around fifteen thousand head of sheep and goats, and about five thousand head of horses. In one of them revolutions down there three years ago, when the *revoltosos* got the best of

80

things for a while, one rebel army of two thousand men all were riding Estrada horses.'

'Just a sort of pore country boy, huh?' grinned Stub, and winked at his brother.

'Sort of,' Bill Allen agreed solemnly. 'Of course, he owns a grain mill in Chihuahua City, along with a big slaughterhouse and an iron works. Come to think of it,' he added, 'I think he once mentioned that he owns the Banco Minero there, too.'

'Holy cow!' marveled Frank Burton. 'No wonder you ride a silver-mounted saddle an' have silver-mounted Mexican spurs. Looks like you're sure in solid, boy!'

To their surprise, Bill shook his head. 'No,' he said slowly, 'it's more than that. It's because of Carmelita, the one I'm going to marry. Right now I'm just kicking up my heels and having a little fun while I'm still free. Once I get married, I'll be taking my place in the family and expected to do my share. Right now I'm waiting for that fool brother of mine to show up. He used to be a scout with General Miles till Geronimo quit last summer. Right now he's a pardner with a man named George Hand in a saloon in Wilcox.'

'Whaaat!'

Stub Burton had popped upright and was standing on his knees, staring. Frank looked as though he couldn't believe what he had heard.

'You say George Hand's saloon in Wilcox?'

'Why, sure. What's eating you fellers now?'

Frank shook his head, chuckling. He said, 'This is the doggonedest thing I ever heard of, Bill. It was in George Hand's saloon that our old man got killed six year ago by a gent named Willie Agens. I killed Willie in the same spot the next day.'

'Yeah?' asked Bill, freezing a little and not knowing what to expect now.

'We're the Burton brothers, Frank and Stub,' Frank said. 'That's why I ain't been back. You ever hear of us?'

Bill Allen didn't reply for a moment, his mind working rapidly, the hope inside him that Ed would show up and show up quick. The three horses still stood dozing as horses always do in shade when the sun is hot, switching lazily at the flies around their heels and flanks. The birds still twittered in the foliage above, the silent waters of the little stream running serenely eastward before turning south again. The sun had crawled its molten way on downward toward the horizon as though wishing to escape the very hellish heat and brightness that it itself generated.

Finally: 'Yes. You see, the old Don runs a freight service into Wilcox about once a week for hardware and stuff that he can't get in Mexico. Some of the American riders working for him go up pretty often, and the old gent himself makes the trip about every ten days or two weeks in his six-horse coach. Whoever is in town has standing orders to go over to the newspaper office and pick up the papers that've been held. We got 'em yesterday.'

'Go on,' prompted Frank, trying to suppress his eagerness. 'What did they say?'

'Nothing about you, if you're asking something special. Just that a couple of Mexican herders working for that German in Colorado got killed up in Apache Basin and that some Texan named Parker was found buried by the sheriff of a place called San Marino.'

'That all?' demanded Stub, openly eager.

'That about summed it up. What got me was that they seemed to be touchy about it all the way down here. I stopped off at an adobe bar back down the creek here a ways, where I bought the mescal, and when I mentioned sheep—meaning Don Alphonso's—some gent down there almost climbed my frame. Well,' he said, rising to his feet, not hastily but with a certain alacrity of movement that meant he was anxious to be out of there, 'I'd better get rolling along to meet Ed. Glad I met you boys.'

83

'Same here, Bill,' Frank replied, also rising. 'I guess we'll drop down by this Alamo place, git a couple of drinks, and be on our way south. Maybe we'll see you down there.'

'Maybe you won't either, you spawn of Satan and black darkness!' thundered Lem Cooley's voice. 'Get yore hands up—all of you!'

Frank Burton wheeled in a flash, and his hand was halfway down to his hip before he stopped the draw and slowly raised his hands. Lem Cooley and Pete Parker, leveled Winchesters in their hands, came up over the bank along which they had crawled for cover. They moved in, the old man's fiercely triumphant eyes glittering with an insane light of more than triumph: a light of unholy joy.

'I said get yer hands up, ye young rat!' he snarled at Bill with a nod of the repeater's muzzle.

'Who's a rat, you old buzzard!' yelped Bill Allen indignantly. 'Why, for two plugged pesos I'd take that blunderbuss away from you and kick the seat of your skinny behind all the way across the creek.'

He had, however, slowly lifted his hands.

There was nothing else to be done.

The two men came up the bank, and their boots made crunching sounds as, six-shooters in hand now, they came up close. 'Get their guns, Pete,' Lem Cooley ordered. 'So you thought you could put somethin' over on old Lem, hey?' sneered the rancher. And to Pete Parker: 'Git their guns while I keep 'em covered, Pete, an' then tie their hands behind 'em.'

'Now look here, mister,' protested Bill Allen. 'I never met these men before until a few minutes ago. I—'

'Shut up!'

'You go to blazes!' retorted Bill angrily. 'I'll talk all I want to. Now you listen to me, you old polecat: I don't care what you got against these two men and them against you. That's your business. But I've never been up in that basin before, and that ain't all. I ain't going, sabe? I didn't lose any sheep or cows up that way and I don't intend to go up hunting any.'

Lem Cooley stood still covering the three now disarmed men, eyeing the courageous youngster in the roll-brim hat with gold lace around the brim and who wore silver-mounted spurs. It was plain that the fierce old man was impressed.

'Where ye from?' he demanded. 'Speak up!'

'Mexico. I work for Don Alphonso Estrada.'

'Yeah? Where ye goin'?'

'To Wilcox. I got a brother up there.'

'Hmmm. We'll see, young feller. I don't

want to do anything to yer if ye don't deserve it. But tie his hands anyhow, Pete, until we git this all straightened out.'

Parker was doing that very thing and making an efficient job of it. Presently the three men stood with their wrists lashed behind them, and Cooley sheathed his six-shooter and rested his rifle upright against a tree. He brought out a plug of black tobacco, bit into it replaced it in a pocket, and spat. He began to chew contentedly.

'Now look here, Lem,' Stub Burton began. 'We don't know what you got against us, but it can't be anything because we ain't done nothin'.'

'Ye don't say. Just a couple of innercent, hard-workin', honest sheephands, heh?'

'He's telling the truth, Lem,' Frank insisted doggedly. 'We ain't done anything to you.'

'It won't do you any good,' cut in Pete Parker angrily, his eyes no longer bloodshot but filled with hatred. 'We found my cousin just a few hours after you swung him. He was still limp when I cut him down and buried him. Your tracks were fresh and easy to foller. You thought you was plumb slippery to split up sixty miles apart, hey? Well . . . you'll find out.'

'What are you goin' to do with us, Lem?'

Frank Burton asked, as though he weren't already certain, for he knew the ways of this fierce-visaged old man only too well. He'd been born on his ranch, been whipped and even kicked by him. He'd seen him kill a man one morning for striking a horse on the nose with a fist. He'd watched him put a loop around a dead Apache's ankle, tie him to the saddle horn, and drag the Indian a mile in order that the stench from the bloated carcass would not permeate the air around the ranch.

Cooley glanced up at the lone limb of the giant cottonwood, and grinned and spat. 'How long did Ron Parker kick after yer swung him?' he asked. 'How much did yer git paid?'

'We didn't get paid aything,' cut in Stub, his voice a little high-pitched now. 'We wasn't workin' for the sheep outfits. We done it because he used to insult us over at San Marino. Called us "greasers" because our mother was a Mexican, and you're married to one yoreself. So we squared up with him, that's all.'

'It ain't goin' to do yer any good to lie,' grunted out Cooley, and wiped at his dirty beard, his jaws working complacently. 'An' don't think thet other feller got away. I put my foreman an' an Apache half-breed trailer on his trail. They had orders to keep after him til they got him, or not to come back. An' ye can bet yer shirts they'll be back,' he added.

Bill Allen shifted, and his big silver-mounted spurs rattled even in the sand. He said, 'It still ain't none of my doing, mister. I told you I'm from Mexico.'

'Now don't git yerself excited, young feller,' grunted Cooley. He opened his mouth, dropped a black wad into one palm, tossed it away and wiped the mouth again with a dirty sleeve.

'I ain't excited,' retorted Bill spiritedly. 'I'm just gettin' sore, that's all. Plenty good and sore. If my brother comes down here and finds me stretching rope, I wouldn't want to make any bets on how long you two will live afterward.'

'Maybe,' Parker cut in in his flat voice, 'we'll hang him, too. You cain't kill one wolf cub an' let the others go. They all come of the same litter.'

Movement came from among the trees, and a small group of men rode into view and swung down in silence. Tony Moreno, the former Reverend Samuel Ernest, Joe Beckum from Texas, and the man Bert. The others had elected to remain behind. They had been sitting and talking shortly after Bill Allen's departure when Cooley and Pete Parker showed up. They'd left the trail of the Burtons and cut a circle to get into the trees and come upon Tony's place.

'A regular audience.' Stub laughed to keep up his nerve 'What some gents won't do to see a good free show.'

Samuel Ernest stepped forward, his pale eyes in the ascetic face upon Stub Burton. He said quietly, 'No, not that, my friend. We were just afraid that something like this—' nodding toward Bill Allen—'might happen, and we came to prevent an injustice.'

CHAPTER ELEVEN

He turned his pale eyes upon the hairy face of the cattleman from Apache Basin. 'This boy is from below the border and has nothing to do with any of this unfortunate trouble.'

'We're all innocent,' Frank insisted doggedly, though his words lacked conviction. 'I tell you—'

'Won't do yer any good, hear me, ye sheep-lovin' whelp. Takin' sheep money to kill a *cowman*! I'm glad yer paw ain't alive to see how low ye've sunk.' He ignored Frank and looked over at Bill, the words not unkind, or as near to being kind as was possible in a man of his nature. 'All right, young feller, tell us ag'in.'

Bill shifted his feet in the sand and tried to twist at the thongs that were cutting off circulation and causing pain in his hands. He said earnestly, 'It's like this, Mr. Cooley. I've been working in Mexico for the past three years for Don Alphonso Estrada. I'm going to marry one of his girls this fall. I was just heading for Wilcox to see my brother Ed when I ran into these fellows. That's all.'

'Hmmm. Ye never was up in Apache Basin, hey?'

Bill shook his head. 'My brother Ed was up there a few times as a scout for General Miles while they were trying to run down Geronimo.'

'Wal, if he was chasin' 'Paches he must be all right, so I guess we better turn ye loose, sonny. Pete, cut him loose, hear me?'

'Gee, thanks, Mr. I—'

'Hold on there, Cooley!' roared Joe Beckum's voice, and the burly-shouldered man strode forward, as the rancher looked up inquiringly. 'He said his brother's name is Ed Allen. I thought there was somethin' familiar about his face. Now I got it! He's from San Saba County, Texas. He's got two more brothers down there, one of them a stinking deputy sheriff. I oughta know, because he arrested me fer hoss—he arrested me, blast him!'

'If he did,' jeered Bill, 'you had it comin'. Mike don't fool around with nothin' but murderers and hoss thieves, you coyote.'

Pete Parker stood behind Bill, indecision in his eyes as he waited for developments. But Lem Cooley merely grunted. He said to Beckum, 'Thet ain't no skin off'n my nose, mister. Thet's fer you an' him to settle. Untie him, Pete.'

'But he's a sheepman!' roared Beckum passionately, waving his hands for emphasis. 'He came in down there a little while ago at Tony's braggin' about how sheep was puttin' cowpunchers an' ranchers out of business up here.'

Tony Moreno's voice cut in sharply, 'Shut up, Beckum. Keep out of something that's none of your business.'

Cooley said to Beckum quietly, 'Go on; what else did he say?'

'He said where he comes from they're running thousands of head. Thought it was funny about sheep comin' down this way. If you want me to go to work for you up there in that war, then swing him!'

Samuel Ernest laid a soft hand on Lem Cooley's arm, the worry in his pale eyes naked and undisguised as he looked at the now fierce-eyed old man. 'Mr. Cooley, this man is

91

trying to use you to settle a personal feud. He's evil. Last year he helped some utter strangers hang a boy from this very tree—the boy buried in that grave over there. He's drunk, his brain inflamed with alcohol. Surely you aren't going to take away an innocent boy's life just because of the evil in this man?'

'Shut up!' snapped back Cooley. 'I got to think a minute.' He looked at Beckum. 'Ye say yer want fightin' pay?'

'Not if that young pup goes free. I got a grudge to settle with his fambly.'

Cooley straightened, shifted the rifle to his other hand. 'All right, mister, yer hired. Pete, go down below the bank an' git the hosses. You, mister,' to Joe Beckum, 'takes them three ropes off these fellers' saddles. So yer like sheep, do ye, young feller? Well . . . we'll fix that!'

He was deaf to the pleas of Ernest and Tony Moreno, both of whom were unarmed. The man Bert stood by in helpless silence, wanting to do what his heart dictated; aware that he was unable to summon enough nerve to try. He'd been a peaceful plodder too long, the middle years having overtaken him and buried once youthful courage under a layer of stolidity too deep and thick to be broken out of now. He heard the pleas of the two other men fall on deaf ears, knew that for months his dreams would be haunted with the knowledge of what he might have done had he but tried.

Pete came spurring back, leading a second horse. Beckum had three lariats coiled on the ground beneath the lone limb of the tree. There was a dead, eerie silence now, broken only by the *whuck* of a rope flopping over the limb, out near the end. Parker dropped it, leaving the two ends dangling, strode over and half flung Frank Burton toward those two dangling ends. The elder Burton said nothing as the loop went around his neck. Cooley shifted the rifle into a position that would brook no last moment interference from the three watchers.

'All right, Pete,' he ordered. 'Git on yer hoss an' dally around the horn. When you git him drawed up, swing over so's this other feller can help ye to tie the rope around the trunk, hear me?'

'You bet I hear you! Now these sons of guns will know how Ron felt just before they swung him.'

He inserted a foot into the stirrup and swung up, wheeled into position, and dallied the dangling end around the horn.

'So long, Frank,' called Stub. 'I'll be up there with you in a minute. And remember, boy, we didn't beg and whine like that Big

Hat Texan, did we?'

Frank Burton's answer was cut off as the cow horse moved forward. His body rose slowly, the legs twisting and drawing up convulsively. When the head was almost up to the limb, Parker wheeled over and rode a half-circle to the trunk where Joe Beckum waited eagerly. It was but the work of a few moments for them to run the rope around the trunk and tie it.

'All right, Stub,' Cooley gritted out savagely, an unholy light in his eyes. 'You coulda been on my ranch today, where you was born, workin' at an honest livin'—'

'At twenty-five a month?' Stub Burton jeered at him. 'When we got two hundred and fifty apiece for swinging thet whining, begging Big Hat? How much did you pay him for shootin' them two Mexican sheepherders in the back? Ten dollars?' He finished with a laugh.

Cooley took two steps forward, his eyes flaming. With plenty of power for his age, he swung a bony fist at Stub's mouth and knocked him down into the sand. Stub lay there, the blood beginning to trickle. There was no fear in him, not even a grunt as the boot toe thudded into his side.

Cooley drew back to kick again and found Samuel Ernest astraddle of Stub's body, protecting him from the raging old man. He said quietly, 'You'll have to kill me if you try that again, Mr. Cooley. This barbaric thing is horrible enough without resorting to added brutality.'

'Get outa my way, preacher. Here, you,' to Beckum, 'haul him up on his feet. Pete, git that other rope over the limb.'

And not more than a minute later Stub Burton's body swung beside that of his brother. There were two ropes around the bole of Hangman's Tree now.

Samuel Ernest stepped over to where Bill Allen, now white-faced, stood waiting. 'I wish there was something I could do for you, Bill,' he said gently. 'But I'm helpless.'

'Not a thing, mister, I guess. But if my brother Ed doesn't show up down here, I wish you'd get word to him in George Hand's saloon in Wilcox. As a scout for General Miles, he knows every foot of that country up there; and him and my two other brothers from Texas will know what to do. So don't worry about this insane old buzzard getting away with anything. He's just putting a noose around his own neck.'

Cooley drew out his plug of tobacco again and bit off another piece. He eyed Samuel Ernest levelly. 'If yer goin' to carry some messages, preacher, ye better tell thet Apache tracker to git some sense an' stay right down here. He comes foolin' up around my country and I'll swing him too, hear me?'

'All right, sheepman,' grunted Beckum, and seized Bill by the shoulders. 'I wouldn't miss this fer anything in the whole world. It oughta make yore deputy brother a whole lot happy to know that Joe Beckum squares his accounts. Parson kin send word to Mike Allen that I'll be plumb happy to have him come up to the basin fer a visit with me. He kin tell him I'll be waitin'—with a rifle. Okay, Pete, get set to dally.'

That was all there was to it, and presently a silent group of men stood looking up at the three figures, turning gently in the slight breeze. All of the group except one. Samuel Ernest stood with head bowed, hands clasped over his chest, his lips moving silently.

'Wal,' Lem Cooley remarked complacently, moving to his horse, 'There's three of 'em I won't have to worry about any more. So I guess thet's all fer this time.'

'Not quite,' Pete Parker suddenly warned, and jerked his own rifle from the saddle boot.

It went to his shoulder and crashed three times. He lowered it and turned to the group, unaware of or ignoring what their faces so plainly said.

'That's what happens when they string up a

Parker from Texas. Well, let's go, boys. I'm hungry, an' the drinks are on me.'

He mounted and followed Cooley off through the trees. The man Bert mounted too, misery plain in his eyes; he was plainly doomed to be haunted for the rest of his life. Tony Moreno looked at Samuel Ernest, a silent question in his own eyes. But Ernest shook his head and indicated that Tony was to follow the others and leave him alone with the three dead men.

The last of the horses disappeared among the trees, leaving only silence except for the twittering of the birds.

CHAPTER TWELVE

At eleven o'clock the night train came in from El Paso on time and clanked to a stop, and Sheriff Carl Boyd got to his feet, shaking awake the man hand-cuffed to his left wrist. He took down his small handbag and a late newspaper and followed his prisoner to the ground where a deputy waited with a rig.

Boyd placed the bag in the back of the rig and then reached for the handcuff key. He was thirty-five, a lean and iron-hard rancher, who'd been away from his family too much these past months since he'd literally been forced into office.

'Take him over to the jail, Tom, and then come back to George Hand's for me,' he ordered the deputy. 'I'm worn out and need a drink before I turn in.'

He strode past the station and up a dark street, carrying the newspaper he'd bought shortly before entraining in El Paso. He was worn out from a six-hundred mile horseback ride trailing a murderer, sleepy from the almost sleepless ride back, anxious to see his wife and children again. Hand's saloon was almost deserted as he stepped in through the back door. Just a couple of men drinking and talking and three more asleep at one of the tables.

Allen was busy counting up the night's receipts and putting them into a canvas bag. He looked up as the sheriff entered.

'Hello, Carl,' he greeted him warmly. 'I heard you were due back tonight. Pretty hard trip?'

'The same kind of a trip that you're going to have in a year when I can get back to my ranch and family and let you take your share of the responsibility,' retorted the sheriff. 'Give me a good stiff one, Ed. I could sleep for a week.'

Allen complied and leaned on the bar as the sheriff drank and then sighed in satisfaction.

He said, 'That's better. Now I can get some sleep and go home for a couple of days, and I don't care if the sheriff's office falls apart. Anything happen while I was away?'

'Not a great deal except that sheep war up in Apache Basin. They killed two herders and hung some cowpuncher named Parker. Paper just printed it here this morning.'

Boyd unrolled the newspaper he carried and laid it on the bar. 'They did more than that. They got another up north. Fellow named Bud Tracy, some hanger-on up there. Cooley's foreman and some half-breed Apache were caught right in the act when they lynched him. They're being held in Prescott for murder.'

Ed picked up the bottle, but the sheriff shook his head and put a palm over the glass. 'One's enough. No sign of the Burtons down this way?'

'None. Your boys have been watching all trains as well as the town.'

'Good. Look, Ed, I'm worn out and I'd like to spend at least a few days out home. How about you taking over as under-sheriff until I get back? You might just as well start learning something about the business now, because you're sure as the devil going to be my successor next election, I'll see to that.'

Allen explained to him about the trip south,

and presently George Hand came waddling in. Allen took off his apron and hung it up on a peg.

'All right, boys,' he said, shaking their shoulders. 'We're about ready to close up. Poke, you better get on home and get some sleep. I mean in a bed. You've got to start loading cattle at daylight.'

He helped them put on their hats, and when they had gone stumblingly and bleary-eyed through the front door, Allen bade the sheriff and Hand good-night and went out into the coolness. His place of abode was a rented cabin not far away, and it was only a matter of minutes until he came out of it with a saddle over one shoulder. He saddled one horse in the small corral, led the other to the front door, brought out the pack and lashed it.

Presently the few lights of the town still visible vanished altogether and he was alone in the desert with a late moon overhead, the night just right for riding. It had been such a night as this when he and two Chiricahua Apache scouts had located Whoa's camp at Buckskin Crossing; and then there had been one whale of a fight at dawn, with bugles blowing, carbines crashing, men yelling and running, and horses shrilling. As usual, Whoa wasn't among the dead or the wounded the soldiers were dispatching; and he remembered

100

the tight anger in Lieutenant Ashford's face the following afternoon when he learned that during the battle Geronimo, whom they'd been hunting, had been burning a ranch one hundred and sixty miles to the south.

Allen picked a well-worn trail and let the animals jog along. At four in the morning he made dry camp, slept three hours, and was on his way again after a breakfast of bacon, cold biscuits, and coffee with canned 'cow' and sugar. He rode all that day, changing horses at regular intervals to make good time.

As men go, there now was little to distinguish him from hundreds of other riders in this vast southwestern cattle country with its burning deserts, yawning canyons, and weird-looking rock formations standing out against the skyline. He wore a brown hat, peaked into a high crown, blue shirt that was a little faded, corduroy pants and scuffed moccasins made by the squaw of a Chiricahua scout. They had doeskin tops and iron-hard rawhide soles. His leather chaps were well-worn and of the 'shotgun' type—that is, pulled on over his boots in the manner of a pair of trousers. Leather fringes went down the sides.

The gun at his hip was a .44 Smith & Wesson with a walnut handle. He preferred it to the heavier .45 caliber Colt worn by many men, because it was somewhat lighter and, therefore, much less uncomfortable to carry, particularly when most of the belt loops were left empty of lead.

Allen's spur rowels were much smaller than average, about half an inch in diameter, and looked very much like a cavalry spur. This because they threw no strain on his leg muscles, holding them away from the sides of a horse, and he didn't need either big or sharp rowels to handle the well-gentled type of horse he now rode. When you were past thirty, your leg muscles and bones began to set, and then was the time to step aside. Let the brash young kids like Bill gleefully sit astride one of the raw ones and take the terrible jolting impact while the animal tried to fling a man apart.

Ed Allen crossed Arroyo Seco and turned south, following the course of the creek as so many earlier day people before him had done. It was almost sundown when, riding south, he reached the bend in the creek and turned east. And still there was no sight of Bill.

'Just about what I figured,' he grinned to himself. 'He didn't get past that Tony fellow's place. He'll probably be sound asleep by the time I get there.'

He thought, Oh, well, it'll probably do the kid good. He's all fixed for life and with no worries about the future. Tomorrow I'll take him off into the hills, and set him to work a couple of days poking around among the hot rocks with a pick. He'll cuss and grumble, but I'll sweat that poison out of him in a hurry.'

The trail widened, and in the coolness beneath the trees where the birds still twittered before settling down for the night, he saw the man ahead of him in a glen.

In the deep sand along the bank of the creek Ed Allen's horses approached at a leisurely walk, and so engrossed was the man working with the shovel at three fresh mounds of dirt that, when he did turn, the stranger was sitting his horse only a few feet away.

'Good evening,' Samuel Ernest greeted Ed in his soft voice. 'I'm afraid that you startled me a bit.'

'I expect your nerves were a bit on edge. I know that mine would have been.'

His eyes were on the three mounds patted down with the back of a shovel, on three ropes coiled up near the graves, on the three extra saddle horses. He raised his head and looked up to where that lone limb, the last one left, was attached to the bosom of the mother trunk that had spawned her spreading brood so long, oh so long ago in the past. Three fresh marks, made by the sawing passage of a rope, were visible. Samuel Ernest spoke, standing

103

there bare-headed, leaning on the shovel.

'Yes, stranger, it was a lynching. Two brothers named Burton, and a third man. Horrible, brutal, barbaric. God's handiwork destroyed by men whose minds are diseased; men without honor, without conscience, without soul. I thought as I stood there watching it that this thing can't be, that this kind of a thing could be expected to happen only among uncivilized men of the dark ages.'

Ed Allen swung down and stretched the saddle kink from his legs. The stoop, the curve of the man's spine, the flat chest—all had told him that this man was from the East. He was unused to these things.

He said dryly, 'Aren't you kind of forgetting that it's been only a year since we finally ran down Geronimo, the last of the Apaches? You've never seen a woman after the Apaches finished with her, did you? You've never seen a man after he's been lashed to a wagon wheel, his eyelids and tongue cut away, his body mutilated? That didn't happen in the dark ages. It happened right here . . . dozens of times.'

'But they are savages. They don't know the meaning of the word God.'

'They knew it before the white man taught them different, taught them to hate. Who did this job here?'

'A man named Cooley, and two other men. Parker and Beckum. And may God have mercy upon those men's callous souls ... if there is any vestige of their souls remaining.'

'Cooley?' repeated Allen. His eyes narrowed. Carl Boyd, the sheriff, and so many others of the people down this way had been afraid that something like this might happen. 'Is he the same Lem Cooley who's fighting the sheepmen up in Apache Basin?'

Ernest nodded and leaned the shovel upright against the huge bole of the ancient cottonwood. He was tired from the physical effort that had drained away much of his strength; his ascetic face was drawn from the ordeal, and from the disappointment of his failure to save Bill Allen's life. He remembered now that young Bill had said his brother was on the way down to meet him. he saw the resemblance to the dead boy in this older man's eyes and aquiline nose above the carefully clipped blond mustache. He waited with an inner dread for the inevitable question, heard the man speak it.

Harshly. Like the lash of a blacksnake whip. 'Who was that third man?'

Ernest cleared his throat and his head dropped as though he couldn't meet the eyes of this man. When he spoke his words were almost a whisper.

'Your brother, Mr. Allen. He was your brother.'

CHAPTER THIRTEEN

He heard the swish of moccasined feet scuffing through the soft sand and watched Ed Allen walk over to the graves and saw the man's hat come off, held in the right hand, over the heart. Ernest walked over and stood beside him.

'I buried him there somewhat apart from the others, Mr. Allen, because he belonged apart from them. As a former minister—my name is Samuel Ernest—I could have done no better spiritually had he been one of my own congregation. And he accepted like a man what the Big Fellow has decreed for him; without fear and without cringing. You see, Mr. Allen, that Big Fellow has a big job to do across the Line and He needs a lot of help. If you'll accept it in that light, it will help much to alleviate the pain of his going.'

Allen put on his hat and looked at the earnest face of the man who himself had come west to die just as young Bill had come west to live. Whatever emotion Ed Allen felt inside of him lay locked up behind his eyes; to remain there until he was alone.

He said, 'The others were the Burtons, you said?'

Ernest nodded and told him the details as the two men walked back to the tree. 'They left the three horses here, knowing that I would remain behind and bring them in later. You see,' he smiled, 'last year a group of strangers came through here in hard pursuit of a young fellow who had just left Tony's place. They caught him and swung him from this same limb, which is why we now call this cottonwood 'Hangman's Tree,' and left him. They said he was guilty of that and more. But guilty or not, he deserved a decent burial and received one. So of course when this horribly unjust thing happened this afternoon, it was expected that I would take care of the final details.'

He began to pick up the ropes and fasten them to the saddles of owners whose roping fingers now were stilled. Allen took Bill's rope and put it on the saddle, smiling quizzically at sight of all the silver; thinking of the kid who had run away five years before and come to Arizona hunting him. The kid who had loved life so much.

He thought, I hope this fellow is right about Bill being called across the Line to help Them out over there. If that theory is true, then

They sure picked Themselves a good hand.

And, grimly, But I'm glad I'm not packing that deputy's badge Carl has been trying to force on me for months.

He finished and looked up to see Ernest with one hand against the trunk of the Hangman's Tree, gazing speculatively upward to where the gashed and weatherbeaten thing pointed a sharp, ugly spear up into the evening sky. He turned to Ed Allen, his fist pounding against the rough bark a couple of times, his pale eyes lit by a strange fire.

'Mr. Allen, I'm going to tell you something that I wouldn't ever mention to the other men because they wouldn't understand, and my words would be greeted by laughter. It may be against the Supreme Laws to believe that there can be anything wicked in inanimate nature, but to me there is something diabolical about this tree. Please don't think me erratic or, as the boys sometimes say, a little off my nut. But ever since this scarred and ugly monstrosity was chosen as an instrument to hang that boy last year, I've had the strange feeling that I should have come up here and chopped it down. Had I done so...' He pointed wordlessly to the three fresh graves. Then: 'They might not be resting there now.'

Ed shrugged tolerantly. Let the man believe what he wished. He merely said, 'They'd only have picked out one or two of the others around here.'

Ernest's eyes gleamed anew. 'Would they, Mr. Allen? Tony and myself were unarmed and helpless. But the third man wasn't. A man named Bert Clifford; a middleaged peaceful man. I could see in his face the desire, the desperate urge to do something. He was trying so hard to get up enough courage to try. A few minutes' delay, a chance to catch them just right, and the miracle I was praying for could have happened. It didn't because I, in my weakness, didn't chop down this diabolical monstrosity. A Devil's finger growing up out of God's wonderful earth from the depths below, beckoning cruelly to men's souls. I'm too tired tonight, but early tomorrow morning this foul thing that has taken the lives of four men crashes to the ground.'

Ed Allen already was swinging up into leather. He felt a deep sense of respect for this strange man's character, a deep sense of gratitude for what he had done for Bill. There let the matter rest. He bent and caught the reins of the red horse bearing the silver-mounted saddle and then took the reins of another horse that had a *cholla* infection lump on one shoulder. To his surprise, Samuel Ernest had not mounted.

Ernest saw the question in his eyes and

smiled up at him. He said gently, 'If you'll just ride down a way and wait for me, I'll be along shortly.'

Allen nodded and set off down the trail, leading the two horses. Fifty yards away he pulled up to a halt and looked back. The man was on his knees, hands clasped to his breast, chin down.

And while he prayed over the graves of three men the eerie silence in the glen was broken by a terrible rush of wings. A big hawk came diving down with the speed of a meteor and crashed through the green foliage among the birds and soared up again with a tiny screaming victim in one yellow talon.

Samuel Ernest raised his head and watched for a moment, then rose to his feet and flashed Ed Allen a strange look that Allen did not understand. The man mounted and came on, leading Frank Burton's horse.

Presently the trail widened enough so that they could ride abreast. It was almost sundown now. Allen finally broke the silence between them.

'You say this fellow Beckum was the cause of Cooley changing his mind?'

'Tragically so. He seemed to bear a personal grudge toward another of your brothers some place in Texas.'

'San Saba County.'

'Yes, that was it. A deputy sheriff, I believe. He mentioned an arrest and almost admitted that it was for horse theft.'

'Sounds like another Willie Agens.'

Ernest gave him a puzzled look. 'I beg your pardon?'

'He was the man who killed the Burton brothers' father. Frank Burton shot him the next day.'

'Ah ... I see. Blood for blood. An eye for an eye, a tooth for a tooth. I don't, of course, subscribe to such beliefs. Of what avail is it, Mr. Allen?'

Ed Allen said, 'It might save somebody else's life, the lives of many others.'

Something like a tired sigh came out of the flat chest of the gaunt, sincere-faced man riding beside the larger man who wore the Apache moccasins.

'Life is a very complex, a very strange thing at times. Take this cattle-sheep war so far away. Two men were killed on one side. Then the opposition retaliated and hung one of their men.'

'Two,' corrected Ed Allen dryly. 'And two more are charged with murder and will get the same thing.'

'And now three more today, one of them innocent. And, following that, you going straight to Tony's place with a bleak look in

111

your eyes and a strong hand above a death-dealing gun.'

Ed Allen reined up and the other man stopped too. Allen slipped the worn .44 from its sheath, opened the loading gate, clicked the empty cylinder from beneath the hammer, and inserted a sixth cartridge. The weapon went back into the sheath.

He said, 'Yes, that's where I'm going, Mr. Ernest. But tomorrow morning you can go ahead and cut down that tree. It won't be needed any more.'

He lifted the reins and looked at the other man again, his face so cold-looking it appeared pale.

'Keep the horses here out of sight until it's all over,' he ordered harshly.

CHAPTER FOURTEEN

Tony Moreno's still pretty but now buxom young wife, left alone with her two boys that afternoon, saw the *viejo barbado*—the bearded old one—finish a final drink and then say he'd best be getting along to get those two men he had trailed so far.

After he and the young one were gone she pleaded with her former *capitan* husband not to follow, to keep out of the troubles of these fierce gringos and attend to his own business. But Tony remained adamant because of his fear that young Bill Allen might become involved, and Tony wanted to make sure nothing happened to a man who was to become the son-in-law of Don Perez y Estrada. After all, Tony had known Don Alphonso quite well, having at one time been stationed at the great hacienda. He had been married there, and Don Alphonso, though clucking his tongue, had been most sympathetic and wished *el capitan* much success in his new life.

So Tony had gone, accompanied by Bert, with Joe Beckum trailing along to, 'see the fun,' as he had expressed it. That left but four men remaining in the place, two homesteaders and two strangers *la Señora* Margarita saw had shifting, uneasy eyes. These four promptly had departed almost upon the heels of the others; the two homesteaders to avoid involvement, the two strangers for obvious reasons: they were wanted by the law and a lynching would bring the law down here as soon as it was notified that the Apache Basin war had gotten out of its designated battleground.

With fear for her husband's safety because she had long since come to know the ways of these violent gringos, she went back into the huge kitchen-dining room to her stove and her two sons toddling around on the hard-packed dirt floor. And the hot food was ready when she heard the sounds of horses. Soon she saw her husband and the *viejo* and the others come tramping in. One look at her husband's drawn mouth and she knew that there had been a tragedy and a terrible one.

Tony came into where she was busy over the stove. He shook his head at her fear-filled face. 'Say nothing, *chamaca* (girl). These three carry guns and are evil. Bert has returned to the ranch, sick and trembling. I'll tell you all later tonight.'

He returned through the doorway in answer to a bellow from Joe Beckum. 'Hey, Tony, come on in here and let's have something to drink. The boss says he's not only tired but thirsty. So'm I.'

Tony poured the drinks for them while his now frightened wife hurriedly began to prepare supper for the three. She placed the meat and beans and fresh corn from her garden on the table, added a plate of hot *tortillas* and a big pot of coffee on top of a flat stone in the center of the rough table. It was late enough now so that her two dozen chickens were trickling in through the back door and taking their places on a corner roost to sit there blinking sleepily and occasionally making deep clucking sounds. They were safe from the coyotes until the good *Señor* Ernesto could finish a rock-floored adobe house that would keep out the digging marauders.

She carried green beans and squash bowls to the table, stepped past a tiny Chihuahua hairless dog asleep on the floor, and from the doorway caught her husband's eye.

Tony said, 'The supper is waiting on the table. I'll eat later.'

They filed in, Lem Cooley removing his hat. None of them bothered to wash at the basin bench out behind the kitchen. Joe Beckum was somewhat sobered up now, though his stomach told him that he'd been drinking and would not forget it right away. Cooley sat down, pulled a hand down over his hairy mouth, and reached for a *tortilla*.

They ate in silence, as hungry men do, while Tony stood in the doorway and waited. Normally he would have eaten with them; but not tonight. Presently Cooley, his hunger partially satiated, began to talk, while Pete Parker and Beckum listened entranced.

Beckum mouthed a piece of *tortilla* and beans and said, chewing. 'That must have been some fight, Lem.'

'No more'n a dozen others like it we had in the old days,' grunted the old man. 'When

115

they got real bad, after the mescal ripened an'
they went on their fall drunk, sometimes
they'd band up together, the hull gang of
different tribes such as Cherry Cows, Warm
Springs, Tontos an' Mescaleros. Then things
got tough. They'd drive every rancher and
homesteader and everybody else outen the
country. Them as was fools enough to stay got
kilt and mutilated; men, women, and kids.
The cavalry would have to go outn' bury what
was left, only the married sojers bein' allowed
to bury the wimmin because they was naked
an' all cut to pieces.

'But there was two of us them blasted bucks
soon learned to let alone. Me and ol' Pete
Kichin, who had a hog ranch down below
Tucson near the border. Didn't take *us* long to
learn 'em a lesson, I can tell ye! Pete sold hams
and lard all over the territory, an' them black
devils used to think it was fun to run by an' fill
them hogs full of arrers just to watch 'em run
around squealin'. Took just about three raids
fer 'em to find out it wasn't so funny. They
found out the same thing up my way in
Apache Basin. I built my ranch an' fought
them mean devils fer twenty-seven year
now—and along comes a danged furriner from
Yurrup who thinks I won't fight. He'll find
out soon enough whether I will.'

He brushed back his stringy grey locks,

which persisted in falling around his face when he bent forward to scoop up the food. He chewed noisily on beef spiked with chili.

Beckum was all agog. He took a big draught of black coffee, the sound of its passage down his gullet like that of a thirsty horse drinking from a trough.

'How many was there the mornin' Victoria made that raid I heard about?' he asked.

Cooley picked up his fork and began to work at a sliver of meat between his few remaining scraggly teeth.

He said, 'Not too many. 'Bout thirty or so, I reckon. I allus had a man up in the bull-pen on top of the house watchin' fer the devils, especially at daylight. They won't fight at night if it kin possibly be helped. The ghosts of their dead ones are roamin' around and cain't be disturbed, ye hear? But them black-skinned devils would come in at daylight an' they'd be right on top of ye before yer could see one of 'em. I rec'leck thet mornin' that Andy Burton was up on top on guard, takin' his turn like all the men did. I'd just got up when I heard Andy's rifle open up an' heard an Apache screech. Then things got under way fast. It was some ruckus, what with the shootin' while the wimmin an' kids huddled out of sight and squalled. Burton's Mexican wife an' two kids, just like them two

117

young'uns right there by the stove. Yep, the same two spawn of the devil I strung up today. An' if I'da knowed they'd turn out like they did, I'da shot the both of them on the spot that mornin'—'

Joe Beckum wanted to listen eagerly to the rest of it, but was too restless to sit still any longer. He pushed back the rawhide and willow chair and rose. The woman was lighting coal oil lamps in the kitchen and barroom, for dusk had come with its cooling hand; a doctor placing coolness on the fevered brow of the desert. Beckum stepped outside. A night owl on an early prowl for a supper of field mice sailed low overhead, and not far away a young burro colt tugged at the milk supply of its mother and swished its short tail in hungry ecstasy.

Beckum strode on rapidly, anxious to get some fresh air in his system and return while the old man still was in a talking mood. A new, sudden impatience gripped him; a strange impatience to get to work again after more than a year of loafing down here in an adobe cabin. To get up into Apache Basin. To get into that war alongside this fighting old man.

He came back almost at once, and then movement a hundred yards away caught his eye. The dim outlines of a horse and rider.

Cooley's new fighting man sprinted for the back door of Tony's place. He stepped inside and looked down at the rancher, who was alternately picking his teeth with the fork and sipping more black coffee.

'Lem, you'd better do something fast,' he said hurriedly. 'There's a rider comin' in just back of the corrals.'

'Wal, what of it?'

'For God's sake, boss! That Allen kid we strung up said as how his brother was due down this way today, and if's as tough as the one who arrested me back in Texas, there's goin' to be some plain and fancy hell popping around here *muy pronto*.'

One thing could be said for Lem Cooley. He didn't appear to be very much upset at the news. He said, 'Yep, I rec'klect now. So it was his younker brother we danced today, heh? Wal, too bad, but he oughta stayed outen bad company. Pete, I've got my back to the bar-room door. You git up beside it. Don't reckon ye'll have too much trouble pullin' his fangs. Joe, yer better wait outside the back door just in case.' He looked at Tony and said mildly, 'If yer try to warn him, mister, it won't be good with ye, hear me?'

Tony nodded woodenly and went back to his place behind the short bar.

He had deserted his God, and now the

scourge of Evil was upon his household and upon his head.

CHAPTER FIFTEEN

Six years now. Six long years since I've seen my homeland. My own home is a nest for the scum of the border because the rust of greed has encrusted my heart; my grandiose plans to fight as a leader of the peons are buried beneath the weight of the gold in my money sacks. Jesus and Mary forgive me! Oh God and Father, what have I done to Thee? The Wind is in the sky, and I am one of the grains of sand roiling before it and turning the bright sun to ochre before the angry lash. The spike I drove into the Cross is staining red my own hands—Oh God and Father, what have I done to Thee?

He heard a scuffing sound as though a rat were scurrying among the mesquite wood piled back of the cook stove. He saw first the Apache moccasins with tiny little spurs at their heels, and then he saw a face he had seen many times but had not known until now. He looked through the open doorway to where Lem Cooley's bony back was visible as the man sat with coffee cup in hand, still gouging at his broken yellow teeth with a tine of the fork.

Tony Moreno started to speak and then clamped his lips tight as Ed Allen strode on past with a nod. He stepped into the doorway, his eyes bright with the kind of brightness seen on the surface of a frozen pond.

'Cooley.'

Just the one word. Lem Cooley twisted around in his rawhide-covered chair and looked up at the man towering above him and four feet away.

'Yep, that's me, young feller. If yer lookin' fer a job with fightn' wages, I ain't hiring down this way. Too much law. Not like it is up whar I come from.'

Allen said, 'I understand you strung up my kid brother this afternoon along with the Burtons.'

'Hmmmm.' Cooley deliberated thoughtfully. 'A young feller, ye say?'

'Did you?' he asked coldly. Waiting, also deliberately.

'Coulda been. Seems I rec'klect there was some young feller along—Pete! What're yer waitin' fer?' he roared.

'Nothing,' came the calm reply. 'I've had him covered from under my left arm. So don't git excited.'

Allen stood there, staring at the muzzle of

the gun, more enraged at himself than frightened. He'd been so sure of himself; sure that they would be tired after sixteen hours in the saddle, full of food and relaxed. He'd hoped this would be sufficient to give him an even break with the three. He hesitated, weighing the decision, remembered there was a third man now not present. He heard Pete Parker's snarled, 'Git yer blasted dirty hands up or I'll blow you apart!' He saw the burly form of a third man come in through the back door with a drawn gun. The man Samuel Ernest had mentioned. Beckum. Allen had served him drinks many times.

Beckum was grinning like a gargoyle as Parker slipped the .44 from Allen's sheath and pushed it into his waist band. He broke into a guffaw.

'This is really somethin', Allen. The dernedest thing I ever heard of. Down in San Saba County in Texas I had trouble with Mike Allen, the deputy. I allus figgered to go back some day and square up. I never thought I'd git the chanct to do it 'way out here in Arizony. Funny, huh?'

Allen's cloud-grey eyes leveled themselves at him steadily. He said, 'To a man of your kind, perhaps. I'd say an unfortunate coincidence to a boy who never harmed you or any other human being in his life, short though it was.'

'I'm going to make it another one of them coincidences and shorten yore life, too,' retorted the fugitive. 'Shore, I know. The sheriff is a friend of yourn and you got two tough brothers back in San Saba County, too. Well, I got one of you today. You make number two. And when the last two come faunchin' out here, I'm going to wipe the slate clean.'

Tony Moreno appeared in the doorway, his black eyes going first to his wife huddled up on a stool in a corner and hugging her two apprehensive boys. Tony had decided, right from the beginning six years before, that he would never have a gun within reach, and that all of his customers, the peaceful and the bad ones, must have made known to them that fact. It would insure his complete neutrality in any quarrels and prove conducive to a much longer span of life.

He had none now either to use or to slip to Bill Allen's oldest brother. But there was no doubt as to his meaning, his determination, when he spoke.

'There will be no murder committed by you in this house,' he stated quietly.

Lem Cooley had risen to his feet and now sat with his buttocks against the edge of the dining table, his legs outstretched lazily.

'Don't aim to at all, Tony,' he replied. 'No doubt about it, it's too bad about that young feller we stretched. Hull trouble now, though, is thet I cain't let this feller here go because he'll be on my tail. Him an' mebbeso his brothers an' friends.'

He looked at Allen, the familiar glitter beginning to appear in his fierce, hawk-like eyes. Ironically, he was still picking at his teeth with the fork. He spat on the hard-packed dirt floor and grinned.

'So ye come bustin' in here to kill old Lem, hey? Wal ... let me tell ye' somethin', young feller, hear me? Durin' the past thutty or forty years they's been a lot wuss men than ye are tried it an' every one of them gents, includin' a hull passel of 'Paches, ain't around any more.'

And to Tony. 'Have yer woman feed him. Pete kin go out an' unsaddle his hoss. I've rid since before daylight an' I'm too tar'd to do anything tonight except put my tarp roll in the front room an' go to sleep. Joe, you been loafin' all day while we been hittin' the trail hard. We'll put this gent where he won't do no harm tonight and you stand guard over him, sabe?'

'Sure thing, Lem. You can sleep sound. I won't let *this* gent get away.'

From the front doorway came the sound of footsteps, and Samuel Ernest came in from

124

out of the darkness. He saw at a glance what had happened and shot Tony a look that might have meant anything. He had waited with the three horses until Allen dismounted in front of the place and then brought them to the corral.

Pete Parker looked at him and grinned. 'Git 'em all buried?' he inquired solicitously.

Ernest nodded silently, remembering the scene at the tree, the sadistic cruelty and hatred this man had displayed. He knew that lynchings were commonplace everyday occurrences; that blood-mad mobs had shot their dead victims, dragged them through the streets, burned them in public squres, making a celebration of such nauseating affairs. But these things had happened far away; his knowledge of them had been acquired only by the lurid accounts written by newspapermen of the day. But this affair. . .

Parker spoke to Lem Cooley. 'We better tie this jasper up, too, Lem. Just because he's a preacher don't mean he might not try something. He shore tried hard enough a little while ago to help another Allen outen a bad hole.'

'I'm a man of peace, Mr. Cooley,' replied the ex-minister. 'This terrible war of retribution you're wreaking upon your enemies one hundred and fifty miles away already has taken its toll of one innocent victim and scarred the lives of others by what they have witnessed. I have no desire to bloody the hands of my Maker with the lives even of men like yourselves. I assure you I do not own a pistol. I would not invoke the use of one did I possess a dozen.'

Cooley apparently was satisfied. He nodded for Ed Allen to sit down at the table, then yawned and stretched. 'Take care of the hosses and such, boys; I'm goin' to sleep.'

Allen sat down at the table and, covered by Beckum's .45 single action, ate a few bites of the food the thoroughly frightened Mexican woman placed before him.

Nobody else had put in an appearance. The doors of the Mexican adobes were closed and barred; the timid occupants who eked out a meager living with their gardens and goats and chickens were huddled inside and crossing themselves. Many bad men they had seen here, *si*. But these were a scourge.

By the time Allen finished eating Parker strolled in from taking care of all the horses. Beckum motioned with his pistol for Ed Allen to get up. 'Out that door, ahead of me.'

There was nothing else to do but comply, and Ed walked ahead of the two men, fear still not clutching his heart; only a bitter sadness at the thought of Bill up there under that blanket of cold, damp sand. He'd have to rest there until word of what happened—to the two of them—reached Carl Boyd. All Carl could do then would be to burn up the wires to San Saba County, Texas, get out a posse, and send a wagon. A wagon with two air-tight boxes.

He shook off these thoughts, flaying himself in excoriation for not thinking of any possible escape. They stopped before a small adobe cabin. While Parker held his gun on the prisoner, Joe Beckum opened the heavy door and lit a lantern inside. The single room, built for a few dollars by some of the Mexicans now locked in their own cabins, was about nine feet square with a flat sod roof. In one corner was a makeshift pallet of straw and smelly blankets that exuded the odor of sweat and the nitrogen of horses. A table of sorts held the smoky globed lantern and a partly empty bottle of colorless mescal. There was a water pail, half full and surfaced with a film of dust; a pair of worn out boots and dirty trousers tossed into another corner.

Beckum smiled and nudged his new crony as Ed Allen looked at the four open windows, a foot in diameter, with canvas flap blinds rolled above. Eye height.

'Portholes, Allen,' the lyncher stated with satisfaction. 'I had the Mexes build 'em just that way, and I don't go out mornings until I look in all directions. A good sheriff don't think nothing of trailing a man across two or three states. And though Beckum ain't my real name, I don't take chances. Not after I stole a man's hoss down San Saba way and Mike Allen arrested me. I made bond and then went out and killed the feller fer complaining to the sheriff. My relatives made bond on that one, too, but when I stopped off on my way out of the country to kill that brother of yourn he wasn't home. So I kept right on going. And so far there ain't nobody showed up lookin' fer me.'

He reached for the door, of hand-hewn cottonwood six inches thick, with a strip of sheet iron bolted on the inside. It was hung on iron hinges bought in Wilcox, and could be heavily barred from the inside nights, and chained from the outside when the owner was gone.

Beckum said, 'I'm padlocking this from the outside, *amigo*. But that ain't all. I'll be sittin' here on the outside with a chair tipped back against the wall, all night. And I'll be wide awake. If I hear any noise like you tryin' to dig out. . .'

He left the rest of it unsaid and closed the door, running the chain through a hole and around the door-jamb of peeled cottonwood. The padlock snapped into place and the man from San Saba County sheathed his pistol. Parker was rolling a cigarette.

'That oughta hold him, Joe. But you keep awake. And keep an eye on thet preacher's cabin, too. I wouldn't trust him an inch, because them guys ain't right in the head. Their ideas are plumb twisted. Take a man like thet, no tellin' what the fool might try. Never trust a crazy man, says I.'

'Don't trust *anybody*, Pete. You better get some shut-eye.'

Parker licked the cigarette into shape, lit it, and strode off toward the corral to get his bed-roll. The man who called himself Joe Beckum settled himself comfortably in the big chair also made by the Mexicans, rolled his own cigarette, and felt content with the world.

CHAPTER SIXTEEN

Inside the *cantina* part of The Alamo the cattle baron of Apache Basin flung his light bed-roll onto the dirt floor and straightened with a tired sigh. It wasn't much of a roll: two blankets for padding, and the tarp only in case of rain. And there was no rain at this time of the year. Depending upon the purpose and speed of a journey, there were many ways you could make up a pack. A slicker roll with frying pan and coffee tin and a few staples lashed back of the cantle. A pack horse diamond hitched with all a man's personal possessions. Or a light pack with only essentials when speed and distance were necessary. Walk, trot, gallop. Stop and dismount. Unbit and graze for just five minutes. Change horses every two hours, water every four hours. A bit of oats when you could get them.

Cooley kicked the roll flat with a booted foot and went over to the short bar. He yawned. 'Gimme a mescal to sleep on, Tony. I'm shore tar'd. Guess I ain't as young as I used ter be.'

'How far did you come today?' asked Samuel Ernest. He was thinking of the sheriff, that he'd want all available information should there be a posse.

Pete Parker came in carrying his own bed-roll, and the canvas covering made a sharp *thwup* on the floor as though a bale of hay had been dropped from the upper story of a storage shed. Tony poured a drink, and then a second for the other man.

'How far? All the way from Stinking Springs. 'Bout sixty mile, I reckon. Them young pups didn't fool me none when we found Pete's cousin Ron swingin' up there in the hills. Not old Lem Cooley who's been fightin' an' trailin' 'Paches for nearly thutty year. I knowed they'd meet up ag'in. All we had to do was hit the trail, an' when it come together ag'in whoever got there fust wait fer the other'n.'

'There was three of 'em,' Pete agreed, and downed the fiery contents of the glass. He drank water and wiped at his mouth. 'And that third one who went north didn't git away either, huh, Lem?'

'No,' cut in the quiet voice of Samuel Ernest. 'He didn't get away, Mr. Cooley. Last night before Allen left Wilcox the sheriff came in on the late train from El Paso with an evening newspaper. It stated that a man named Bud Tracy had been lynched, that a man named Casey and a half-breed Apache Indian with him are being held in Prescott on charges of murder. Allen told me about it this afternoon.'

Cooley gave off an oath and almost glared at the ex-minister. He wheeled on Pete Parker and cursed again. Then without a word he half flung his empty glass on the bar and went to his bed. He sat down and removed his boots, and the odor of his damp socks could be smelled in the room. He glared again.

'Pete, I'm older'n you, so yer let me sleep two three hours, then wake me up. I don't trust these fellers.'

A grunt went out of his angular frame as he rolled over with his face to the opposite wall. Another muttered curse came to the ears of the three men. 'Casey an' Half-Breed Carlos, heh? Like fun they'll keep 'em in jail. Ain't no men of mine bein' hung fer swingin' the killer of a *cowman*.'

Samuel Ernest straightened from his lax position at the end of the bar. Tony had brought in a pan of warm water and was washing with soap all glasses used during the day. One of the children in the kitchen was whimpering fretfully, tired after a long day of playing in and out of the room. That unknown instinct which causes a child to feel and share the same emotions as a parent has had filled the boy with the same fear that permeated his mother. She placed him on a pallet in a corner near the curled up figures of his older brother and the sleeping Chihuahua pup. On their roosts the safely protected chickens blinked and made noises deep in their throats.

Samuel Ernest said, 'I believe that I'll go to my cabin, eat some supper, and rest, Tony. I'll see you early in the morning. It's been a very trying day.'

'I'll be locking the front door in a few minutes myself, Sam. We'll sleep in the kitchen on pallets tonight. Good night, Sam, and may Our Lady of Guadalupe forgive us the sins we committed this day, and look over us until the coming of a new dawn.'

Pete Parker said ominously, 'I don't know about anybody *else* lookin' after you tonight, Preacher, but you can bet yer shirt that there's somebody on the job. Joe Beckum. He's keepin' an eye on that cabin of yourn just like we're keepin' an eye here. You'll be pertected plenty just as long as you don't go walkin' around in yer sleep, sabe?'

Ernest paid no attention to the significant remarks. He was looking at Tony. 'You haven't deserted Him as much as you imagine, Tony. One thing about that: when it penetrates your mind and settles there, no matter how great your defection some of it always remains. *Verdad*? Good night, Tony.'

'You ain't said good night to *me*,' jeered Pete Parker, and then guffawed at his own sharp wit.

The darkness outside was cool to Ernest's face as he made his way through the soft sand toward his tidy cabin about seventy-five yards distant. He saw a pinpoint glow of red light up briefly in silhouette the face of Beckum.

'That you, Preacher? Better sleep tight tonight. I might git nervous an' start shooting if I see some gent strolling around where he ain't got no business.'

Samuel Ernest made no reply but walked on to his cabin about thirty or forty yards farther on. He went inside and lit the lamp, the yellow glow lighting up the white-washed walls, the home-made furniture, the neat little kitchen. On the rock and mortar stove with the sheet iron over the top he found stew and cold Dutch Oven biscuits. Later he sat down on the two clean sheets between which he slept during summers and read a nightly chapter from the Bible. After a prayer for the soul of young Bill Allen and the two Burtons, he slept fitfully through the night.

He arose and dressed before dawn the following morning, as was his custom, and went first to the open door to peer out. Beckum's figure was still in the rawhide chair where the man often loafed in the shade of his crude and dirty cabin. Ernest saw it stir and hope died in him. Beckum was not asleep, had remained awake all night.

*   *   *

Inside the cabin, Ed Allen had slept a few short hours, because he'd had little rest since two days before. Outside the cabin, Joe Beckum got up, yawning, and stretched gruntingly. He took a turn around the cabin and, without peering through into the

134

darkness, knew that his prisoner was still safely secured inside. He was licking his dry lips in anticipation of a morning drink when he saw Samuel Ernest come out of his cabin and stroll toward him. Ernest had an ax over one shoulder.

'Mawnin', Preacher,' drawled the outlaw blandly. 'Goin' someplace?'

'I am.'

'Kind of early to be out choppin' wood, Sam. Besides, I allus thought yore woodpile was out back of yore cabin,' baited Beckum.

Ernest ignored him and strode on toward the corrals. Beckum stepped out two paces, his face beginning to harden. 'Sam, you come here,' he ordered.

Ernest saw what was in the man's eyes and walked over, the ax still over a shoulder. Beckum said, 'Sam, I come from a purty big and wealthy family back in San Saba County in Texas. They're hard-workin', God-fearing people. All except me, who didn't cotton to the ways of the rest of the folks. I've known you fer a year, and I know you mean well and all that. But you ain't cutting down that cottonwood tree where we strung up them three yesterday. So you can just stay right here with me until Tony and his missus gets breakfast. As soon as we get rid of Allen we'll be pulling out of here for Apache Basin to finish up the job old Lem started against that sheep outfit. So just put down that ax and then go roust 'em out over at Tony's. And bring me back a glass of mescal.'

Ernest put down the ax, leaning it against the wall beside the chair. He said quietly, 'God didn't intend for me to be an errand boy for men of your kind, Joe. If you want it, you go get it for yourself.'

'And leave you to chop a hole through the wall with that ax? You think I'm crazy? Oh, I almost forgot.'

He turned to the small window and peered into the darkness. 'Hey, Allen? Allen, you awake?'

'What do you want?'

'Awake, huh? Did you drink up all thet mescal of mine last night? All right then, pass it through. I'm thirsty.'

He heard stirring from within and the sounds of fumbling around in the darkness. The lantern rattled, and then he heard the clink of the bottle being knocked over on the table.

'Don't spill it,' snapped Beckum impatiently. 'Leave enough for a good snort.'

Allen's voice said through the narrow opening in the adobe wall, 'Here it is, and I hope it chokes you.'

Beckum chuckled and reached for it. A

hand with fingers of steel snapped out through the opening and fastened onto his right wrist, a second shooting through and locking around his throat. Beckum flailed helplessly, gurgling, and tried to reach over with his left hand and secure his gun. The weapon, however, was snatched from the sheath, and then Samuel Ernest raised the barrel high. It thudded hard and then thudded again. Beckum sagged, held up by the strength of Ed Allen's wrists resting on the sill.

'It's all right; you can turn him loose,' the former Reverend Samuel Ernest said softly. 'I didn't know how hard to strike him. You see, I've never had much experience. I hope he's not dead.'

'Not his kind, Ernest. His skull's too thick. Get his keys, quick.'

Ernest obeyed with alacrity, experiencing again in a matter of moments something new in his life. It accounted for the awkwardness with which he rifled Beckum's pockets. He unlocked the padlock and cringed inwardly as the chain rattled loudly in the grey dawn. The door swung in and Allen, bareheaded, stepped out and grabbed the pistol. Chapless now, his moccasins made little sound as he sprinted for the back door of the Moreno kitchen.

He leaped through—and collided headlong with Pete Parker, on his way to the outhouse.

Both men went down on the hard-packed dirt floor, Parker's startled yell mingling with the screams of Tony's wife and the shrill yelps of the Chihuahua. The children began to cry.

Allen had dropped the gun when his right elbow struck hard, a shock of pain telling him the bone had suffered injury. He rolled over and grabbed for Parker's gun wrist, slugging at the man's face, a message pounding frantically into his brain to get him fast, that Cooley would be up off his bed with a gun in his hand. That the man would kill and kill quickly.

They writhed there, grunting reserve strength into each straining movement; two men with iron-hard bodies in a fight for life. Mrs. Moreno had the crying children huddled in a corner, Tony was in the doorway, and Lem Cooley was roaring to his feet. Somebody leaped over the two fighting men on the floor and Allen, gripping Parker's gun wrist with one hand while he slugged blows at the man's face with the other, realized sickeningly that he was losing; that time, precious seconds, was running out. Alone, he could choke Parker into submission with his right hand, but . . . he seized the long hair and began to slam the back of Parker's head against the floor. Three, four, five times; then he gambled and let go and grabbed for his own gun. He snapped erect and wheeled toward the doorway.

And then he relaxed and a long sigh broke from his lungs.

The former Reverend Samuel Ernest, pole-ax raised high, stood above old Lem Cooley and dared the cursing old man to make a move.

Ed Allen bent above Parker's struggling form and took the man's gun. Parker was bleeding at the nose, a thin trickle that he kept wiping at with a sleeve. He came to his feet, reeling a bit, and blew his nose and spat.

'Get in the other room,' Allen ordered, a gun in each hand, and shoved the man forward with the hard rawhide sole of an Apache moccasin. And to Tony: 'Take this gun and cover them, Tony, while I run out and find Beckum.'

'With the greatest of pleasure, *amigo*. There was a time when, as a Mexican army officer, I was a very handy man with a pistol. I don't think I've forgotten.'

Allen leaped out through the opened front door and sped back across the sand. He found Beckum sitting up, head bent forward, hands clasped to his face. The outlaw was shaking his head from side to side and spitting, still unable to figure out where he was or what had happened. In his inexperience, Samuel Ernest had done a most effective job, one that would have brought approval to the eyes of a professional mugger.

CHAPTER SEVENTEEN

Beckum lifted his pain-filled face and stared up stupidly at the man who stood spraddle-legged in front of him, a .45 Colt dangling in one hand. His head cleared a bit, and he spat and then rubbed fingers up and down his throat where other steel fingers had left their marks of pain.

'I said I hoped that it would choke you,' Ed Allen told him. 'Now get up.'

Joe Beckum twisted over and got dully to his feet. Under the nod of the gun barrel, he began a shambling walk toward the front door of The Alamo. The roaring pain still lashed through his skull, and his throat ached. For the first time in his hard, murderous way of life he was experiencing a thing called retribution. He had ladled out many times much punishment of his own brand. It had never occurred to him that some day the dark bread would return upon the waters of fate or chance or whatever a man wanted to call it.

He went inside and saw Cooley and Pete

Parker sitting in chairs against the kitchen wall. Samuel Ernest in silence placed another one, but not beside Cooley. The vicious old Apache killer was cursing as few men had been heard to curse, his face contorted.

'You scum!' he almost screeched. 'You dirty—border scum! The first time in nearly fifty years thet anybody ever put one over on old Lem Cooley, and it had to be on account o'...'

It went on for five minutes, the ravings of an old man with a murder-twisted mind whose code of: *Take what you want, fight to hold it, kill without mercy*, had been breached for the first time.

Tony, leaning idly at the open end of the bar, gun in hand, twisted his head long enough to look at Samuel Ernest. 'Looks like Our Lady did what I asked of her last night, Sam, eh?' And there was a smile on the dark, still quite handsome features.

'Looks to me,' was the smiling retort, 'as though you'd better take that as an indication of something very important you said you'd strayed from.'

Tony looked at Ed Allen and chuckled. 'Look who's talking! He goes out and whacks a man over the head with a six-shooter and then comes in to preach a sermon.'

'Cut out the funny stuff an' gimme a drink,'

snarled Joe Beckum, still rubbing his Adam's apple. 'A big one. Or are you too good to serve me now?' he sneered.

'Not at all, Joe, not at all,' was the pleasant reply. 'And no charge for this one, unless you wish to put it on Mr. Cooley's account.'

'Then put it on! It was him got me in this mess in the first place. If he hadn't come down here chasin' them . . .'

That, too, ended in a tirade, and to Ed Allen it was growing a little disgustingly boring. Three years with Generals Crook and Miles as a scout had inured him to a kind of violence unparalleled in history; he had experience burying the victims of Apache atrocities. Although a single man, he'd helped the officers to bury the stripped, mutilated bodies of women, the young girls with beribboned pigtails missing; the bodies of men hanging head down from a wagon wheel and stave, a ring of dead ashes below their white and gaping skulls. These things the soldiers and the civilian white scouts accepted as a matter of fact because the word Apache meant 'enemy'—enemy of all mankind, and with no quarter given, not even among themselves.

Allen remembered the rather pompous British general staff officer who'd been sent first to Africa to study British reverses at the hands of the Zulus and then been hurried to the American frontier to observe the methods of fighting savages out here, this to be reported back to the home office as quickly as possible.

Asked what would happen if the American Indian ever came into combat with the African Zulu, the pompous representative of His Majesty's Government had replied, 'My deah Colonel, the Sioux or your Cheyenne would whip them. As for your Apache, he'd *exterminate* them!'

These things Ed Allen could understand. What these three men had done revolted him.

He said to Ernest, 'If you'll go out and saddle the horses while Mrs. Moreno fixes breakfast, I'd like to get under way as soon as possible.'

'Want to git it over with, huh?' sneered Pete Parker. 'Swing us like we swung them, eh?'

Allen ignored him and went into the kitchen where Tony's wife nodded in answer to words spoken in Spanish. By the time the sun was an hour in the sky and already beginning to turn hot, Allen was ready to go.

He looked down at Tony, at Mrs. Moreno and the two young boys watching from the doorway. Back of him, hands lashed to saddle horns, their horses hooked together by ropes, sat three sullen, now silent men.

Cooley had, by turns, threatened, cursed, offered money, reasoned and then pleaded himself hoarse to a stony-faced man who finally had tired of it and told him to shut up. There was no doubt in his mind as to what was in store for him and where it would take place. Ed Allen would square up for the death of his brother by killing him in the same manner Bill had died.

Allen said, 'Much obliged for what you've done, Tony. Next time you're in Wilcox, drop in at our place.'

'I'll be glad to, Ed. And I don't think I'll go along this time. I had enough yesterday.'

Ed grinned wryly in reply. He hadn't told any of them what he intended to do, that he was heading straight for Wilcox and Carl Boyd's office. There was no reason for him to take personal vengeance now, not even with a six-shooter. The law would do that, beyond any doubt. But he wanted to keep alive in the minds of the three prisoners as long as possible the thought that he intended leaving them hanging at Hangman's Tree.

The little cavalcade stretched into motion single file and began to move past the corrals and the scattered cabins whose frightened occupants had not even yet dared to emerge. Samuel Ernest brought up the rear, leading Ed's pack horse, pole-ax resting over one

144

shoulder. On top of the pack the silver on Bill's saddle struck back flashes from the sun. The birds were in full twitter again in the early morning coolness, and the air beneath the cottonwoods exuded a tang that made a man feel that it was good to be alive, and free.

Heading the six-horse string out in single file, Allen pushed along, sometimes at a walk and then jogging the line into a trot. Impatience was gripping him to get on; to reach the point where they could leave Arroyo Seco and start that burning but final leg of the journey into Wilcox. He and Carl Boyd the sheriff and the other people there had hoped fervently that this thing in the Basin country would localize itself and have no reverberations down here in the desert where, now that the Apaches were finished, men were at peace and building for a solid future. But it had come, and Bill was dead, and now the end was in sight.

Joe Beckum and Parker were passing banter back and forth; coarse jokes to bolster up their courage as Hangman's Tree came nearer and nearer.

'I got sixteen dollars outa my last check from the folks that says I kick longer than you do, Pete,' offered Beckum, riding in the middle and looking back at Parker, who was last of the prisoners.

Parker guffawed. 'I'm broke, but I'll tell you what I'll do: I'll try to git Lem to loan me enough outa my next month's pay. Hey, Lem, how about it? Joe an' me got a bet on to see who kicks the longest. Lemme have sixteen slugs til payday.'

Cooley cursed them roundly and then cursed again at their coarse bawls of laughter. He said to Ed Allen, 'I've seen a few men git hung in my day, an' it's allus the loud talkers who whine the loudest.'

'Let them have their fun, Mr. Cooley.' Allen shrugged, their loud jests covering the sound of his own words. 'They've got a long ride ahead of them. To Wilcox.'

'Yer mean,' demanded the old man incredulously, 'yer ain't-a-goin' to swing us where we hung thet young'-un with the Burtons?'

'Settling matters with a gun when the other man is armed is not murder in a case like this, Mr. Cooley. Hanging is.'

'Hmmm. Never seen sech a queer feller with sech fool notions. But I'm glad, young feller. More than ye might think. I can beat this case in court.'

'You may not get a chance to.'

He had been watching the dust cloud behind a rocky hummock where the desert sloped up in a series of swells. He had wanted to make sure, and now he saw them. Not more than half a mile away. Eight of them, and coming hard.

Cooley saw them too. His eyes flickered to those of Allen; the same thought was in both minds. *Sheepmen!*

Ed Allen swung his mount's head, and a roar to the others broke from him. 'Gig those horses! *Gig them!*'

He slammed the tiny spur rowels into his own mount and came around in a pop-the-whip snap that caused Parker's horse almost to lose its footing. And then they were breaking away, back down the trail beneath the cottonwoods, thundering through the sand. Rocketing back to Tony Moreno's and the protection of thick adobe walls. To their ears came faint yells.

The eight sheepmen were running their horses and saddle mules hard, and behind them the yellow desert dust roiled up and then hung motionless on a yellow morning as Ed Allen rode desperately to save the lives of his three prisoners.

Guns began to boom. Guns from a distance of seven hundred yards. And Allen, remembering the familiar sound of the old .45–70–550 Springfields and what that huge 550-grain slug of lead could do at that distance in case of a hit, twisted his head and yelled back at the three bound men to swing up side by side for more slack rope among the four hard-running horses.

They made a strange group that morning, those three prisoners now riding their panting horses side by side and the captor who rode to the fore with a lead rope on Cooley's mount. Allen fought his hard-running horse with the spurs, knowing that these bound men were doing the same. They who had been his captives now looked to him to save their lives from the sheepmen, who apparently had ridden and trailed them as relentlessly as Cooley and Parker had followed the tracks of the Burton brothers.

Allen drove on, eyes on those hard-spurring men out there coming down from the slope of the desert. There was no thought in his mind of using his rifle in an attempt to make them sheer off. It would be futile and a waste of ammunition. Men who had trailed Cooley so grimly this far hardly would let a few stray shots thrown in their direction by one man swerve them from a race that was going to be close.

Allen looked back over his shoulder. Three hard-running horses. Bobbing noses almost touching the pumping haunches of his own laboring mount. Three men, hats gone in the dust, riding with hands bound and watching

148

those out there in the desert. Hearing the boom of their rifles. Just one stray hit, one stumble of a horse, and the others tied together would all be down in a kicking, screaming mass. And one *other* horseman—a black-robed one riding above, with a scythe over a bony shoulder—would be the victor.

Tony's corrals loomed up, and Tony was in the doorway, listening to the gunfire. 'A knife, Tony!' roared Ed Allen. 'A sharp knife, and quick!'

They hauled up in dust, the barrels of the horses heaving and leather creaking, and Allen jerked his repeater from the scabbard as Tony, acting instinctively, leaped in and cut the bonds of the three prisoners.

'Get inside!' Ed Allen ordered them. 'Bar the doors, Tony. I've got a fight on my hands.'

Tony hurriedly slammed the door as the four men jumped inside, and old Lem Cooley began to roar. 'Where's our rifles an' six-shooters? What the blazes did yer do with 'em?'

Allen's voice rang out harshly, a six-shooter in his other hand. 'No guns, Cooley, and you'll obey orders. I'll kill the first man who refuses. Understand?'

'Anything you say, mister,' Beckum almost croaked. 'Gawd, but that was a close 'un. I could almost feel 'em breathin' down my neck. I need a drink.'

'You won't get one,' snapped Tony, pulling Beckum's own rifle and shell belt from beneath the bar. 'And you keep out from here, sabe?'

Ed Allen said, 'Tony, you take the kitchen with your wife and children. Put Cooley and Parker at the table in the corner out of line of fire. Shoot either one of them if they try anything. You have good enough reason to. I'll hold the front with Beckum.'

'Okay, Ed. What do you think happened to Sam?'

'We had to leave him fast. He's all right . . . I hope.'

CHAPTER EIGHTEEN

Ernest was indeed all right. He'd sat there in surprise as the four others wheeled around and the firing began. He saw the riders and understood. Sheepmen after Lem Cooley. He sighed a bit and himself swung around to follow the others at a brisk pace, apprehension and a silent prayer deep in his soul. He had intended to ride only as far as Hangman's Tree with the party and then turn over the

150

pack horse, Ed having confided that he had no intention of lynching his three prisoners. Ernest had planned to spend the morning chopping down that monstrosity, pack his belongings overnight, and the following morning begin the first leg of his journey back to his home, a parish, the work of his God.

He rode on, and within a matter of minutes they broke through among the cottonwoods and barred his path: seven hairy-faced, tough-looking Mexicans and one Anglo with the hardest face and the coldest eyes of any man he had ever seen. Eight blocking his trail. Ominously.

'Who're you?' snapped out Halliburton. 'Talk up!'

Ernest explained, noting the field glasses on the man's saddle, and added mildly, 'I shan't ask your name, but it's obvious where you came from. You're involved in the Apache Basin sheep and cattle war with Mr. Cooley, aren't you?'

'You're blamed right we're mixed up in it. To a finish. He killed a couple of our herders.'

'He hired a man to do it,' was the mild reply. 'A man named Ron Parker. And then you hired the two Burton brothers and another man named, I believe, Bud Tracy to hang Parker, which they did.'

'Well?' snapped back the sheep foreman.

Back of him sat seven hairy-faced men, some mounted on mules. Black as Apaches, eyes like almond-shaped chunks of coal, Winchesters and Sharps in their hands. Tough fighters that Johnathan Breuger had brought in from Chihuahua as herders. Men unafraid of anything that walked. Four of them were brothers named Mariscal.

Samuel Ernest said, 'So Cooley came down here, riding hard on the trail of the Burtons, who were fleeing to sanctuary in Mexico.'

'Well, dammit, speak up!'

'My friend,' was the gentle reply, 'they didn't get there.'

He told in detail what had taken place the afternoon before, of young Bill Allen, of the older Allen capturing the three. Halliburton shifted his weight in the saddle and spoke rapidly in Spanish, explaining. Out on the desert another rider hove into view, driving a pack mule with their supplies. They had been unable to make the creek the night before, had dry-camped far out in the desert, and started on the trail again long before daylight.

Halliburton looked at Samuel Ernest and grunted. 'Anyhow, we got 'em hemmed in. Too bad about the Burtons. But I don't think we'll need them any more after today. I'm going to surround this place with rifles. Then I want you to take a message in to Allen. Tell him I've no grudge against him. On the contrary. But if he tries to defend those men, I'll have to consider him as one of them. I'm going to get those three if I have to tear down the adobe walls of that place.'

'There is a woman and her two children in there,' Ernest said.

'Then tell them to get out! Okay, mister, get going.'

He wheeled around again and began to give orders to the hairy-faced herders. They scattered in a long circle to surround the place toward which Ernest now was riding and leading the pack horse. At the corrals he swung down leisurely, tied the two animals, and walked toward the front door. It opened before him, closed again, and Tony dropped the bar back into place.

Ernest said, 'I have a message for you, Ed.'

'I guessed as much. Cooley says the man in charge is Halliburton, the sheep superintendent, and that he's about as tough as they come. What did he have to say, though I can about guess?'

'It probably would be right. I explained to them what had taken place. Mr. Halliburton says he has nothing against you as long as you don't try to defend your prisoners. Otherwise, if you do, he suggests that Mrs. Moreno and the children be sent from the house.'

'That's for me to decide, Sam,' Tony spoke up. 'I still own this place and, like a lot of other people in this country, I'm getting a little sore about the whole deal. I might not be the most upright kind of a citizen according to certain standards, but this is still my home and, like Ed here, I'm caught up in something that these men have no right to do. You go back and tell that arrogant gentleman that as an ex-officer of the Mexican Army I used to put the whip to the backs of men like he's got with him. Tell him that these prisoners will not be given up, and that if he tries to assault this place he'll get himself killed.'

Ernest looked a question at Allen, received a nod. 'That's right, Sam. Tell this man Halliburton exactly that. And that these men are being taken to Wilcox and turned over to the law.'

The former minister went to the front door, waited while Tony unbarred it, and stepped out into the morning sun again. For some reason, he thought, it looks yellow this morning. A red yellow.

He picked up the reins of Allen's horse and led the string of them down to the corral and tied them beside the other two. Halliburton stepped into view around the corner of a shed, a Winchester in his hand.

'Well?' he asked harshly.

'I'm putting the horses out of the line of gunfire, Mr. Halliburton,' was the reply. 'Allen and Tony Moreno refuse your demands: Tony on the grounds that you're storming his home and endangering his wife and children; Allen because he refuses to give up prisoners to be lynched. I'll remain with you as a possible go-between in the hope that this thing can be settled without further bloodshed. There's been too much of it already.'

'Not enough,' was the curt reply. 'You're going to see some more.'

He raised his repeater and drove a .44–40–200 slug of lead through the window where one end of the bar abutted the wall beside it, and from the cottonwoods and underbrush all around the house came a seven-man chorus.

The fight—later referred to as 'The Battle of The Alamo'—was on.

Ed Allen ducked instinctively as the slug shattered a window pane at an angle and threw a spurt of adobe dust from the east wall. Beckum, beneath it, sneezed and cursed and crawled along the floor to safer haven. Tony had brought windows from Wilcox for only the front and the kitchen, the east and west walls being solid. Ed knew that those points were safe; that even though gunners crawled up to them, about all they could do, unless

155

they had dynamite, would be to hunker there and wait for a dash from the house.

Tony had picked up the powerful field glasses he used both to watch for the liquor-smuggling pack trains and to scan approaching riders, particularly occasional small groups of Mexican cavalry trailing bandits into Arizona, permission of the U. S. Cavalry. The slugs were drumming through steadily now; not a waste of too much ammunition, of which Halliburton had packed in plenty, and necessary to keep the defenders pinned down. Tony's terrified wife and his children were huddled down back of the big stove, the baby crying with its mother, the older crying to see the fight. Parker had affected an air of nonchalance and was smoking a cigarette when he called coarse jests to Joe Beckum.

'Hey, Joe! Still want to make that bet?' he jeered.

'Go to tarnation,' coughed back Beckum. 'I'm chokin' in this dust.'

There came a lull, and Halliburton's harsh voice came from over back of the sheds, clear through the now shattered and gaping front window.

'Come out of there, Allen! Bring those men out and there'll be no trouble.'

'They go to Wilcox, mister. This is not

Apache Basin.'

'We've got plenty of water and you haven't. Come out of there!'

'We can drink mescal,' haw-hawed Pete Parker. 'Let 'em come in an' git us. Me ... I'm enjoying this.'

Tony was using the glasses now, Joe Beckum's old fashioned .50-caliber Sharps rifle beside him. He caught a glimpse of two hairy-faced men down in the underbrush along the creek, reached for the Sharps, and then suddenly swung the glasses back to the spot. A grin unseen by the others split his handsome face. He grinned again and fired.

CHAPTER NINETEEN

All that morning and into the afternoon the fight continued, having settled down into desultory firing on each side. Halliburton was impatient to get it over with and be on his way back to Apache Basin to send word to Breuger that the war was over and won. But he now knew the caliber of at least one of the two defenders, also the futility of rushing men behind adobe walls and barred doors. He'd found a pair of blacksmith pinchers, used to clip the split edges of a horse's hoof before rasping and shoeing. He was sitting with his back to the wall of the shed, busily engaged in extracting the projectiles from a half-hundred heavy-caliber cartridges and pouring the powder into a tin can. Samuel Ernest watched in silence as the sweating Mexican packer worked over his cooking fires.

Halliburton looked up from his work, and a hard grin flitted across his unshaved face. 'You don't like it, do you, preacher?'

'I'm thinking of the woman and her children.'

'They had their chance, mister. If I can crawl up alongside of that wall tonight below the front window and toss in this can filled with pebbles, they'll come out. Or be packed out.'

'I could go tell them.'

'You fool! They'd be waiting. Probably outside.'

One of the herders made a dash out of the under brush and sprinted for the protection of the wall of the shed. He leaned his rifle against it and removed the Chihuahua hat and wiped at his hairy face.

'Anything new, Pedro?'

'Nothing, *señor*. Nobody hurt so far. Maybe they run out of water pretty soon, eh?'

Halliburton gave a wrench at a 550–grain slug of lead, tossed it aside and grunted as he poured 70 grains of black powder into the can on top of a layer of pebbles. He said, 'They'd better hope it does.'

The herder began wolfing the food. Ernest sat in silence. Halliburton picked up another cartridge from a pile in the sand beside him. A shot spanged out from a point somewhere over to the east and there came the answering roar of a .50–caliber Sharps from the kitchen window.

Tony jerked out the smoking shell, blew through the now greasy breech, and slipped in three inches of cold brass and lead. He looked at his wife to give her assurance. She pointed to the big wooden pail on a shelf above her head. A slug had drummed in through the window following Tony's shot and drilled a furry hole four inches above the bottom. The hole was wet, but there was no trickle.

In the front room where the bar was, the white-washed walls were scarred and gouged, speckled brown like a bird's egg where the white had been shot away. Allen crouched in front of the bar now, changing to a position back of it at regular intervals to stop any possible rush from either direction.

Tony called out from the kitchen, 'Hit any yet, Ed?'

'I haven't been trying to, Tony. This is not my war.'

'The devil it hain't!' roared old man Cooley. 'You'll find out what it is if Halliburton ever gits his hands on ye, yer damned fool. Hell of a note,' he snorted angrily. 'One man who won't hit 'em an' another who couldn't hit a burro at fifty paces.'

Tony ignored him, using the glasses again, and Cooley winked at Beckum and jerked his head. Beckum let out a yell of fright and dived behind the bar.

He came up with a six-shooter in each hand and leaped for the doorway to the kitchen.

Cooley's claw-like hand caught the tossed Colt, and Beckum wheeled on Ed Allen's back, the click of the hammer drowned in the noise. 'Drop that gun, Allen! Get 'em up!'

Ed Allen turned, saw the unwavering muzzle of the Colt lined at his midriff, and slowly obeyed. His face was blank, emotionless. He said, 'All right, mister. It's your show.'

Cooley had leaped forward and snatched up the Sharps and handed it to Pete Parker. That diabolical light was in his eyes again. This was the way it should have been all along. They were Apaches out there under Victoria, and this was his fortress-like castle, and those two squalling kids on the floor were the Burtons.

'Stop them bawlin' brats!' he roared at Margarita. 'You, Tony, git over there where I was. Now I'll show yer some fightin'. Joe, bring me a drink!'

'Wait till I git this bottle uncorked. I've been spitting sand all day.'

The fighting took on a sudden intensity, and almost at once there came a scream of pain from down in the underbrush north of the house. Pete Parker yelled gleefully and jerked the smoke-wisping Sharps back through the window. 'One down. Eight more to go,' he called. 'We'll clean Halliburton and his Mexes outa here in no time. Then we'll finish up things in style. And that,' he sneered at Tony, 'means you this time, *señor!*'

Late in the afternoon Halliburton called for a surrender and was answered with curses. Curses in dry, cracked voices; for the mescal had made its demands and there was no more water to be had. The bullet-punctured wooden bucket was dry.

Cooley strode over to Tony and glared down at him, sitting at the table with Allen. 'Now you listen to me, mister,' he snarled. 'You have that woman of yern plug them holes with wood pegs an' go git us some water, hear me? If she don't come back you an' them two squallin' brats ain't goin' to be here when she finally does, savvy?'

Tony said tonelessly, helplessly, 'Halliburton doesn't care about me or the two

161

children either, Mr. Cooley. He's just as determined and just as merciless toward his enemies as you are. Why use innocent people to help you in your fight? I'm the man who's been defending you, remember?'

Cooley bit into a corner of the black plug and snorted from behind one bulging cheek. 'Defendin' me! Ye think I ain't got eyes? Ye wasn't tryin' to hit them fellers because they're yer own color. Yer think I wasn't married to one of 'em for nigh unto fifty year? Pah! Git her out there, mister.'

Beckum called from the front room, 'Hey, Lem, here comes Sam with a white rag tied on a stick.'

'Let 'im come. Ye come back here an' watch this end. I'll do the powwowin'.'

He moved into the other room, crouching low, alert for trickery. There was none. Ernest walked up through the deep sand and came to a stop ten feet away. He said, 'I can't come any closer, Mr. Cooley. There is a rifle trained on my back and I must speak loud enough for Mr. Halliburton to hear.'

'Wal?'

'Halliburton's herders don't like the idea of the woman and the two youngsters remaining in there any longer. They know you must be short of water. He asks you to let them leave.'

Cooley cursed and spat tobacco juice.

162

'Tender-hearted, huh? Any time thet—' an epithet '—gits all upset over a woman an' a couple of brats, I git the fishy eye. He wasn't botherin' about them durin' the past eight-nine hours. How come all of a sudden now? Uh-huh, Preacher.'

'You refuse?'

'*Absolutamente!*'

'In heaven's name, man! Haven't you any—'

'Nope. None a-tall. Lost it forty year ago. Now you listen to me, hear me? I'm sendin' thet woman out to the well to git us a couple of buckets of water. I'm keepin' them two squallin', thirsty brats here. If she don't git back with it she hain't goin' to have any brats an' she hain't goin' to have any husband either—that is, if they ever got married in the fust place.'

'And that's your final answer?'

'Thet's my answer to a blasted sheepman!'

Ernest turned and made his way back toward the corral and to the corner of the shed where Halliburton waited. The man said, 'I heard.'

He held an odd-looking object in one hand. It was a large rusty tin can that had been filled two thirds full with black powder and carefully selected gravel rock the same size as buckshot. The top had been carefully crimped

163

in, and from it protruded a long thick powder fuse of cloth strips carefully sealed with bacon grease. His hard eyes bored into those of Samuel Ernest.

'You said that yesterday there was another man at that lynching?'

Ernest nodded. 'A cowpuncher named Bert Clifford, who got sick and went back to the ranch.'

'And word went to the sheriff in Wilcox as fast as a man could get there? There might be a posse boiling in here any moment. So I can't hold off any longer. Come over here!'

Two of the Mexicans had finished eating and were crowding around, curiosity in their black eyes. Halliburton knelt and smoothed a small area of sand and drew a rectangle on it with a stick.

'There's the building. Right?' At Ernest's nod he went on. 'Take this stick and draw me a diagram of the wall that separates the kitchen from the bar. Put in the door and where the grub table is.'

Ernest complied, and the sheepman studied it carefully.

Then his face lit up and he whistled softly. 'So that's it,' he said. 'Why didn't I think of it before? Where would that woman and those two kids be, mister?'

Samuel Ernest took the twig and pointed.

164

'In the near corner, huddled up by the big stove here. Away from the doorway. And since Mr. Cooley had a gun in his hand, I know that he's overpowered the other two men. They should be in the corner on the opposite side of the door, both out of line of the blast.'

Halliburton got up, his hard face less harsh now. He was grinning a bit as he spoke rapid Spanish to the two herders, who promptly loped afoot into the brush and began to circle. They were shouting loud; loud enough for their *compañeros* to hear.

Lem Cooley was drinking from a mescal bottle and cursing his burning throat, though he was not drunk. He hadn't overheard, but suddenly Tony stiffened. He and Ed Allen were sitting exactly where Samuel Ernest had figured. Tony leaned over and whispered, 'Get set, Ed. Here it comes. A bomb through the front window. It'll be loud, but we won't get hurt by the blast coming through the kitchen door.'

He motioned behind Pete Parker's back to his wife to huddle down closer back of the stove and to cover the children with her body. Outside, it was suddenly quiet. Too quiet.

CHAPTER TWENTY

Beckum came in from the kitchen, wiping at his now parched lips. 'We got to have some water, Lem. That mescal is burnin' up my insides. I'm on fire.'

'Yer watch this front winder,' the old man replied grimly. 'I'll get us some water. They're holding off, I reckon, after I told thet Halliburton a thing or two he won't fergit.' He strode into the kitchen, snapped the bucket from the shelf, and handed it to Tony.

'Yer whittle two pegs fer them holes an' do it quick,' he ordered harshly. 'They've stopped shootin' while the woman goes after some water fer us. Hurry it up!'

Tony obeyed with surprising alacrity. It was the work of moments to pick up two sticks and point them with a butcher knife and drive them into the two bullet holes. He wanted his wife out of there when the bomb came. He was praying she wouldn't be leaving the back door when it was tossed.

She rose to her feet obediently, leaving the two crying youngsters, and Pete Parker opened the back door. Tony had taken his place with the children to protect them with his body.

And then things happened all at once. Tony's wife saw a Mexican crawling around the front corner below the window with a smoking object in one hand, and screamed. Through the window came the tin can with a short fuse hissing burning sparks from black powder. And Joe Beckum let out a sound that was part roar and part scream. He wheeled and bolted for the kitchen door, screaming, 'A bomb. They got a bomb!'

He leaped through in panic, and Peter Parker followed him. A riata sang out and snapped Parker off his feet. There was a rush of dark faces, and Beckum was down. Ed Allen leaped toward Lem Cooley's back and knocked him through and then rolled aside as a booming roar came from the front room and a huge cloud of dust and smoke mushroomed through the kitchen and out the back door. Through it came Tony with a child holding onto each hand; into the confusion of struggling, cursing men, while a cold-eyed sheepman stood by with a gun in each hand. Halliburton.

Things became quiet again presently. Cooley and his two men, their few hours of freedom over, again were bound; this time in the custody of a man who had seven good men and another with an arm in a sling to back him up. Tony and his wife were inside the

167

barroom, eyeing the broken bottles, the walls and ceilings which now were more brown than white. Dust was still seeping out of the open front door and the gaping front window. Tony left his family and went back outside.

Halliburton was speaking to his men in Spanish, and Allen noted that they also were talking to Tony, but Ed paid no heed because his thoughts were on how he could save these men. He was hoping that Bert Clifford, the man Tony had mentioned, would burn the breeze in a night run to Carl Boyd's ranch fifteen miles south of Wilcox and tell the tired sheriff what had happened. By some miracle Boyd might burn the breeze back with a posse of his cowpunchers and stop the impending tragedy. Halliburton must be stalled somehow.

But Allen had reckoned with a man whose mind was as sharp as his own. He was shooting rapid-fire Spanish at his men. 'Get your horses as quickly as possible and let's go. This is a bad country for us now. We'll not be safe until we're back among our sheep.'

Allen said, 'Mr. Halliburton, the sheriff of this county, Carl Boyd, has just returned from Texas with a prisoner that he trailed on horseback for more than six hundred miles. It took him weeks, but he got him. As long as you kept your war up in Apache Basin, it was

168

out of his jurisdiction and in San Marino. My advice to you is to turn yourselves over to him.'

'Nobody is asking for your advice, mister,' came the cool reply. 'You underestimate the power of a man like Johnathan Breuger. Insofar as grazing rights up there are concerned, he has the law on his side straight from Washington, because it's public land. And he has the money to hire a hundred or five hundred men to back him up and show what those rights mean to a good businessman. As long as advice is being passed around freely, let me give some to you to pass on to your friend, this so-called competent sheriff. Tell him that if he comes faunching up around Apache Basin with a posse, somebody else will get themselves killed. I'm putting an end to this feud this evening. I'm doing it my way, and if you or this Moreno fellow try to stop me, you're wasting your time. Nothing short of a United States Cavalry troop can do that today.'

He issued more sharp orders, and the three men, their hands again bound, were taken back to the same horses they had ridden and were forced to mount. In a matter of minutes the entire group was on their way to the Hangman's Tree. Allen rode his horse and led the other carrying Bill's silver-mounted saddle. Ernest rode beside him; Tony was on the other side. The three of them brought up the rear.

They came at last into the glen with its mighty tree and that lone limb, the three fresh graves and an older one. Beneath the great limb the Mexicans halted the three prisoners and threw two ropes overhead. Allen and Tony and Samuel Ernest sat their own mounts some distance away.

Allen said, 'I wish there was some way I could save them, Tony.'

Tony said, 'I can.'

Ed swung on him in surprise, but Tony blocked the look with a shake of his head. 'Not this time, Ed. They invaded my home, those three. They threatened my wife and children and myself. They showed no mercy, and they shall receive none from me now.'

They swung Pete Parker first, in close to the bole; putting the noose snugly around his neck and then whipping his horse from beneath him. Parker hung there twisting and turning while Joe Beckum sat almost beside him, hands bound behind his back, his bloated face and dry mouth working, his eyes terror-stricken. He was a far different man from the Beckum of yesterday. He began to beg, and his words brought laughter from the herders and a grunt of contempt from

Halliburton.

One of the others led Cooley's horse a bit forward while the fierce-faced old man sat stonily, his eyes straight ahead and unblinking, and Ed Allen wondered what could be going through the mind of such an old man who had fought and killed without mercy for fifty years. Whatever his thoughts, they were never expressed. Lem Cooley slid backward out of the saddle without speaking a word.

'All right, hurry it up,' Halliburton ordered his men. 'Get that third rope over and out further on the limb. We've got to get out of here and travel fast. Might be a posse of *oficiales* in here any moment. *La ley*. The law.'

Then the third rope went over the limb with a sharp *whuck* and Beckum, speechless and pale, his Adam's apple pumping up and down as he swallowed convulsively, felt the noose go over his neck. There came the slash of a quirt on a horse's rump, a startled snort as the animal leaped forward in pain, and Joe Beckum's two hundred pounds of weight hit the rope. The limb bounced up and down twice before that first crack came like a pop of a giant blacksnake whip. The crack came again, and a dozen pairs of eyes looked upward as the sound grew louder.

And then with a terrible, crashing roar the

last limb of the Hangman's Tree came crashing down and the booming roar went rolling off across the creek, up the slope of the desert, to be swallowed up in the heat waves still dancing across the sand and rocks.

A great cloud of sandy dust mushroomed out and blotted everything from view while the horses snorted and turned away from the enveloping wave. Halliburton rode around and, with his men, came to a stop in front of Allen, Tony Moreno, and the ex-minister.

Halliburton said, 'Well, boys, this ends the Apache Basin war. Cooley wanted a fight and he got it. It's all over now and there'll be peace for us all. No more dead men.'

'I think,' Tony Moreno's voice cut in softly, 'that you've overlooked one thing, Mr. Halliburton. You haven't paid yet.'

Halliburton's tension, eased by the end of the chase, allowed him to break into a soft laugh. 'You mean a posse? I've got eight boys and one cripple who can whip off any posse that follows us.'

'Correction, Mr. Halliburton,' came the equally soft reply. 'You haven't any men.'

He snapped out a sharp order in Spanish, and the results were startling. Those grim, bearded Chihuahua herders snapped up their rifles, and Halliburton sat stunned as he looked down the muzzles.

'What the devil is this anyhow?' he roared.

'They're some of my boys, Mr. Halliburton. You're to be turned over to Allen here to be taken to Wilcox and tried for murder. I don't have to tell you where you'll end up. Disarm him and tie his hands!' he snapped out to the herders.

'*Si, mi General. Si, si!*' came a half-dozen voices, and eight men moved in on their foreman.

Halliburton sat there, hands bound, unable to comprehend yet just how it had happened. He shot an oath in Spanish at Pedro Mariscal, *segundo* and eldest of the four brothers. Then came a question. He was answered by a Mexican shrug.

'*Señor* Halliburton, six years ago *El Capitan* Antonio Moreno left the military and came to help us poor peons fight for liberty. He was our general. He risked everything that me and my brothers and others like us could have a better life. Now he says that if we stay here with you we get the same as these men. He says he has much money and that he's going back to Mexico to lead us again. All of us are going back to follow him and fight.'

He shrugged again, and silence followed in the wake of his gesture.

A few minutes later Ed sat his saddle, with Halliburton's horse and the pack mount bearing Bill's silver-mounted saddle on lead ropes. It would be an all-night ride to Carl Boyd's ranch. Samuel Ernest, ax over his shoulder, walked over and looked up. He was smiling.

'I'll finish up here tomorrow, Ed, and be on my way to Wilcox. Back to take up my work again. I'll see you in town.'

Ed Allen nodded, but his eyes were on Tony who rode over. Tony too was smiling. He leaned from the saddle and shook hands. 'It's goodbye, Ed, but a friendship not to be forgotten. Watch the newspapers, because when I get organized we're going to give 'em what for. All except Don Alphonso.'

'Good luck, Tony,' Allen said.

He rode away from the place with his prisoner, heading back toward the life he had laid out ahead in a careful blueprint. Behind him in the glen the Hangman's Tree stood alone, limbless, a great, scarred monstrosity pointing its spear-shaped top into the evening sky. All was quiet now.

The only sound was the ringing blow of an ax.

Photoset, printed and bound in Great Britain by REDWOOD BURN LIMITED, Trowbridge, Wiltshire